LONESOME POINT

Also by Ian Vasquez

IN THE HEAT

⌟ *Ian Vasquez* ⌞

LONESOME
⌐ POINT ⌐

MINOTAUR BOOKS

NEW YORK

F
VAS

This is a work of fiction. All of the characters, organizations, and events portrayed in this novel are either products of the author's imagination or are used fictitiously.

www.minotaurbooks.com

Library of Congress Cataloging-in-Publication Data

Vasquez, Ian, 1966–
  Lonesome point / Ian Vasquez. — 1st ed.
      p. cm.
    ISBN-13: 978-0-312-37810-3
    ISBN-10: 0-312-37810-6
  1. Brothers—Fiction.   2. Florida—Fiction.   I. Title.
  PS3622.A828L66   2009
  813'.6—dc22
                                        2009004514

First Edition: June 2009

10 9 8 7 6 5 4 3 2 1

For Pamela,
of course

Acknowledgments

The talents and patience of others helped to give this story its final shape. Immense gratitude and much respect to my agent, Markus Hoffmann, for his close readings and honest feedback; my editor, Kelley Ragland, for her timely insight; and my copy editor, Dave Cole, for smoothing the story's rough edges.

EARLY IN THE MORNING under a daylight moon, they saw the Reverend facedown in the shallows, black hair afloat, arms outstretched like a Jesus. They pulled him out of the seaweeds and flopped him onto his back, the man big-bellied and naked from the waist down. The crowd of onlookers surged forward for a closer view, a few boys in prom suits hopping onto car hoods and peering over heads. Another Belize City Police Land Rover drove up and two more cops got out and walked over to the group standing around the body.

Across the clearing on a small rise, Leo Varela sat behind the wheel of his father's BMW in a rumpled gray suit, a wilted carnation stuck in a buttonhole. He watched the cops talking, occasionally pointing. His eyes were bleary and he reeked of rum and Cokes. Patrick, his older brother, was in pajamas in the other front seat, exhaling morning breath through the open window. Freddy Robinson was in the back rolling a joint, glancing up every ten seconds and asking them for the play-by-play.

All around, St. John's boys in prom suits sat or stood on car hoods watching. Most of them had taken their dates home hours ago, then had flocked to Lonesome Point after they heard.

One of the policemen turned and studied the swarm of cars. He spoke to another cop, a tall black man, and within seconds they were marching across the clearing ordering everybody to leave, roll out. Boys stood up with defiant slowness and ambled around to get into their cars, start them up. The tall black cop sauntered up the rise to the BMW—Alfonso Robinson, Freddy's cousin. Strolling over to Patrick's window now. He put his hands on the roof, ducked down. "Time to go home to Mommy."

Patrick said, "Hey, man, Leo woke me, told me what happened. It's really the Rev?"

"Indeed. Ugly scene." The cop twisted around to face it.

Leo leaned across his brother's lap. "What happened to him, Fonso?"

"Got shot. Took one in the skull, two in the back." Fonso shook his head. "Man had no drawers on or nothin'."

Cars filled with St. John's boys drove past, some of the boys throwing up waves to Leo and Freddy.

"So tell me," Patrick said, "where's the Rev's car?"

Fonso said, "Well," and spat off to the side. "Assuming the Rev came here in his car, looks like somebody stole it."

Leo gazed across the clearing to the cops standing around the body, silty waves washing up on the hard sand. Seaweed and pebbles and driftwood littered the beach to where it turned west and petered out near a bank of mangroves. It was beginning to sink in: The Reverend was dead, a family friend, a man he'd known nearly all his life.

Fonso said, "You guys best get on outta here." He tilted his head to the rear. "Before the inspector starts crawling up my ass."

They drove away through the open barbed-wire gate, the grand entrance to this ragged beach people had used for years for every illicit pleasure imaginable. In the eighties, a developer had cleared this land, eight miles up the Northern Highway, dredged canals, and started building concrete homes. Then he went broke or was in prison for embezzlement in Panama, Leo forgot which, and now the land was the public's to enjoy despite a gigantic no trespassing sign out front.

Back on the Northern, Leo kept his mind on the Reverend lying there with no pants, his skin looking like rubber. Freddy pulled out his Bic to spark the joint, but Patrick turned around and glared. "Not in the car, dude." In the rearview, Leo saw Freddy tuck the joint behind his ear.

They were approaching the turn to Independence Park, Freddy's neighborhood, and Leo sped toward it, his eyelids getting heavy, the long night catching up to him. He turned right onto the dirt street, steered around rain puddles and deep potholes. High grass crowded both sides, ramshackle wooden houses set back in weedy yards.

"Drop me off here by these brothas," Freddy said.

A small group of teens was hanging out in front of a corner store, a couple of them leaning on bicycles. They watched with surly cool as the car pulled up.

Freddy got out and slammed the door shut, maybe a touch too hard for Patrick's liking. "Yo, listen, Lee," bending at the waist to look through Patrick's window. "We'll party again soon?"

"Course. I don't leave for another two weeks."

Freddy grinned. "My boy. Off to fuckin' college and shit. Somebody pinch my black ass."

"What can I say, accidents happen."

Freddy reached in across Patrick and bumped fists with Leo. He pulled out and looked at Patrick. "Nice jammies. Got any with fire engines on them? That'd look cute. Or Superman?"

Patrick turned his face to the windshield, hit the button and the car window slid up.

A minute later, Patrick said, "You really should be happy you're leaving, know that?"

"How so?"

Patrick sighed. "Well, for one, just that you couldn't do any worse than hanging around that loser."

Leo opened his mouth to say something, thought better of it. He and Patrick would probably never understand each other.

Near the city, Leo thought again about the Reverend and got his mind off that by thinking about Celina instead.

Remembering her look of surprise when he'd shown her his old notebook full of long prose poems. How he smiled when she said, *I didn't know this about you.* Then, last night, kissing her by the Fort George Hotel pool when the prom was winding down. The taste of her tongue, like rum and Coke, only more intense and sweeter. Her shiny black hair like a curtain that hid their kisses.

He pushed the car up to sixty-five, seventy. They tore down the road, only a couple of cars heading the other way so early in the morning. They flashed by the toilet paper factory and the truck depot. Flew by the propane gas plant and the old Texaco station, and coming up now on the left was Varela & Sons. The largest used car dealership in the country. Whenever his father bragged about that, Leo would think, Yeah, Dad, that's because most of those cars jammed in that clay yard behind that high chain-link, beside that three-story glass building that doesn't really suit third-world Belize—most of those cars are stolen; and everybody knows.

And that's why Leo would be content never to see Varela & Sons again.

They were coming into the city, curving around the circular onto Princess Margaret Drive, and Leo felt relieved that he was almost home and just days away from *leaving* home, setting out on his own. His shoulders relaxed. He lifted his foot off the gas and cruised. "You going to tell Dad?"

When Patrick made no reply, Leo turned his head to look at him.

His brother had gone ghost-white. Hunched over, hugging himself.

Leo looked away.

Yeah, it must be hitting Patrick now, the cold shock that somebody had murdered the Reverend. Their father's right-hand man.

THE
KILLING
BOOK I

I

WALKING DOWN A PSYCH WARD HALLWAY in Miami, Leo Varela discovered the meaning of life, but by the time he reached the door leading out, he had forgotten what it was.

He recently started telling people this to watch their reaction, especially someone he didn't know well. He'd say it usually at a bar, or a party whenever the conversation turned faintly philosophical, say it with a straight face. There'd be a pause, and then he'd smile to let them know he was only joking. But he relished that second of silence, the curiosity on their faces.

What Leo didn't say: He worked the night shift on the third floor of Jefferson Memorial Hospital's mental health annex, and several times a night he walked the floor doing rounds and a couple of times truly enlightening ideas *had* revealed themselves, but when he hit the door at the end of the long hall, he'd forgotten them. That's what happens when you're stoned.

Leo wasn't stoned at the moment. Just a little buzzed. Three pulls on a roach at the start of the shift, nothing more than that. He felt mellow strolling the dark hallway, closing the room doors, telling the new patient in Room 307—checking his clipboard quickly—Turn off the lights, please, Mrs. Delgado, it's time to go to sleep.

A fat, naked Haitian woman trudged out of the women's bathroom, a towel wrapped around her head. She stopped to slurp water from the fountain.

Leo raised his voice down the hall, "Hey, Adelia, put some clothes on, please. Or go to your room, whichever. You know you shouldn't be walking 'round here like that."

Adelia looked up, bent down to slurp some more.

Leo walked past her, writing on the rounds board. When he turned around she was crossing to her room, and he was grateful the lights were out. No need to lose his appetite for a midnight snack. He visited the women's bathroom, that and the men's being the only patient areas lit at night. He picked towels off the floor, dumped them in the clothes hamper. Looked behind the curtains of the shower stalls. Nobody sleeping there.

He scanned the rounds board. Nineteen patients, nearly a full house. One in seclusion, the rest in their rooms, except for Adelia. He jotted *H* next to her name (hallway), *A* next to Mrs. Delgado's name (awake), *SR* for Herman Massani (seclusion room), and for the sixteen others an *S* (for what he wished he was at home doing).

In the nurses' station, Rose, the night nurse, asked him, "What break do you want? I'm down for the first, if nobody minds."

Leo said, "The second." He turned to Martin, the other mental health technician. "Unless you want the second. . . ."

"I'll take the last. I had a good rest today." Martin was at the desk preparing patients' charts for the next day. Mindless work: filling the charts with paperwork, checking off boxes, signing your name, over and over. Martin was new on staff, so Leo happily gave him the practice.

Leo wheeled the geriatric chair from the TV room into the hallway, parked it a couple of feet from the nurses' station and covered it with a sheet. He slipped his sweatshirt on. The floor was kept freezing at night under the belief that it encouraged patients to sleep. Leo cracked back the gerri chair; with feet up and his writing pad in hand he could relax and maintain a watch on both the men's and the women's sides of the floor. Oh, how rough the night shift could be.

He'd gotten nowhere with his latest poem. He stared at the line he'd written almost two days before and hadn't the foggiest what would come next. Moments like this made him wonder if he was a phony, how a handful of published poems didn't mean jack when you sat down to write again. You're *not* a poet and you don't know it. Or maybe he did know. He'd not published in almost two years, couldn't even place a poem in one of those obscure literary journals that paid in free copies. At least he wasn't writing about Belize anymore and the mistakes he'd made and all that mess he'd said farewell to years ago. At least he could count that as a success.

Time to look for some inspiration. He turned to the door. "Hey, Martin, I'm heading out for a quick cigarette."

Martin came to take his place in the chair.

Leo headed down the hall to the women's side, opened the door with a key and stepped out into the warm stairwell. He trotted up to the fifth floor, where a plastic chair waited by the window. The fifth-floor ward had closed down a couple of years back so there was nobody around to spy on him. Leo took a plastic baggie from his pocket, and from the baggie he removed a book of matches and a roach. He sparked it. Sucked deep and held that potent smoke in his lungs. Repeated the process, then blotted the stub against the window frame, smoke curling from his lips.

Man, it was a warm night. Middle of February and the heat wouldn't let up. But he was beginning to feel comfortable, all sweet inside. He turned a lazy gaze out the window to the parking lot below. He watched the gate rise and two cars pull out and head up Twelfth Avenue, probably evening-shift nurses going home. Where he wanted to be. In bed with Tessa. . . . He sat back, let his thoughts wander.

Something across the street caught his attention, somebody standing under the lamppost, a black guy in a suit, staring up at the building. Leo observed him awhile. The man glanced at his watch and glided on, until he was out of sight. Odd. Jefferson Memorial smack in a rough neighborhood like this and a guy in a suit strolling the streets so late?

The intercom crackled, and Leo thought, Shit, here we go.

"Stat team to Crisis. Stat team to Crisis."

Leo sighed, gathered himself, popped a Dentyne into his mouth. Last thing he wanted to do right now was deal with some wacko the cops were bringing in fresh off the street.

Martin was already slipping on latex gloves when Leo reached the nurses' station.

Leo said, "You got this one?"

Rose said, "I'd prefer if you go with him. Since he's new."

Leo said, "You sure?" Knowing hospital policy required at least two staff members on the floor at all times.

Rose nodded and said to Martin, "For now just stand back and watch the other techs, okay? Only get involved if they need you. See how they do it first."

"It's highly complex," Leo said. "One must employ keen observation."

Rose rolled her eyes and swiveled the chair back to the desk.

Going out the door, Leo told Martin, "Every call from Crisis Intervention is considered a red code. Been on a red yet?"

"A couple blues only."

"Expect anything on a red. Like they told you in training."

Out in the lobby they waited for the elevator. The door behind them had a small window with iron mesh inside the glass, and beside it was a red phone with no dial or buttons. Above it was a sign:

> Visitors must pick up the telephone.
> Wait for staff to open door.
> Please watch for patients trying to elope.

Leo jabbed the down arrow two more times. "Probably giving trouble again. We might have to take the stairs." Or so he hoped. Then the door slid open and he braced himself before they entered. The door closed, the elevator jerked and started down, and Leo's mouth went dry.

For years he'd been working on his claustrophobia and just couldn't beat it. He'd improved his ability to manage it, but the fear never went away completely. He stared at the floor. And this was the elevator that gave trouble, too. Martin asked him a question, but he couldn't answer. Until he stepped out into the cold, sweet air of the ground-floor lobby.

"No, I've never been hurt on a call." He swallowed, inhaled deeply. "I mean, except for a sprained finger or a couple bruises, I haven't been injured or anything. Guy on the fourth floor, day-shift nurse? Patient broke his jaw a few weeks back."

"I heard about that. Hey, you okay?"

They walked around the corner, past a few despondent-looking souls slumped in chairs. "Yeah, why?"

Martin shrugged. "You look . . . kinda pale. You sure you're okay?"

"Course I'm sure," an edge to his voice. He opened the door to Crisis Intervention. "After you," leveling his tone. They went in, a few disheveled people watching the TV in a high corner, or gazing into space. Leo lowered his voice. "People here, people outside, they're waiting to see the triage nurse." He pointed to an empty Plexiglas booth set diagonally in one corner. "That's triage. The nurse is away from the desk right now but she's the person who interviews them, sees if they require hospitalization. Now, this door here, we don't have a key for it. We've got keys for all other entrances but not for Crisis." He hit a button on the wall, and a few seconds later a tech in green scrubs opened one side of the double doors.

At the end of the bright hallway two uniformed cops with empty holsters stood next to a bare-chested Hispanic man with hands cuffed behind him. Leo led Martin past the nurses' station and conference rooms. Two techs from Crisis joined them and by the time they reached the cops, techs from other floors were streaming in, tugging on latex gloves.

"The goon squad," one of the cops said, smiling at them.

Nobody smiled back. Pablo, the Crisis night-shift head nurse, asked him, "So who do we have here?"

"This here is Reynaldo Rivera. Reynaldo was dashing across

I-95 traffic, no shoes, dressed like this. Said he was just waiting for a cab, isn't that right, Reynaldo?"

The bare-chested man grunted. His feet were filthy and he smelled swampish.

Pablo said, "You know if he has a history?"

"Used to be a patient at Locktown Community Mental Health Center, he says."

"That's Dr. Burton," a female nurse standing by said. "He'll be here in the morning."

Pablo gestured to the group of techs. "Let's take him in the back."

Two techs held Reynaldo by the upper arms while the cops uncuffed him. Then they led him to a door with a huge window, while another tech opened the door with a key. They guided him into an area surrounded by seclusion rooms, big Plexiglas windows in all the doors. In a couple of the rooms patients were sleeping, restrained to their beds.

The nurse hurried ahead with a sheet to a vacant room, tossed the sheet over the bed, tucked it in. They undressed Reynaldo quickly, slipped on hospital pajamas. Before they laid him down, they gave the restraints a tug to make sure they were buckled tight to the bed. They slapped them around Reynaldo's wrists and ankles, started locking them with keys.

Reynaldo jerked a leg loose and stamped wildly, catching a tech on the shoulder. Another tech leaped onto the leg, trying to hold it fast to the bed. Reynaldo reared up as far as he could, bucking, neck veins bulging, face red. "Let me go, mothafuckas, I didn't do nothin'! Let me go!"

"Easy there, easy," Pablo said.

Leo and another tech grabbed ahold of Reynaldo's arms and pushed him back down.

His wrists pulled at the restraints. "Don't do this to me, I'm innocent!"

A nurse rushed in with a syringe, dragged his pajama pants down and stuck the needle in a thigh.

Reynaldo bucked a few more times, swinging his head from side to side. Leo turned his face away, sensing what was coming.

Reynaldo spat. Leo felt some on his neck. The techs at the feet released him and backed out of the room, Leo and the other tech following, the next gob splattering against glass as they slammed the door.

Walking back outside, Leo wiped himself down with a paper towel and said to Martin, "See how they get? The second they know you're not gonna hurt 'em, when they feel the worst you have is four-point restraints, they lash out. Happens all the time, just be careful." Leo nodded in greeting as they passed the other techs chatting in a loose circle, peeling off gloves and dumping them in a wastebasket.

Martin said, "You're not going back up?"

Leo had stopped by the lobby doors outside Crisis. "Just a quick smoke. Tell Rose I'll be up in five."

The night air felt comfortable after the arctic chill inside. Leo walked the curb past the Crisis police entrance, where a big red sign said NO FIREARMS ALLOWED BEYOND THIS POINT.

He stopped by the gate to the parking lot and smoked a cigarette, only his third for the day. He'd been cutting back for the last four years. He figured that by age fifty he should have his habit licked, or cancer. He preferred the go-slow attitude in most things. Maybe that's why he was still at Jefferson two years after he'd declared the job a dead end. He looked up at the sky, a few stars dim in the city lights. He thought one day real soon he'd have to make some life changes, with a baby on the way, bills growing, his career options shrinking as he grew older. Man, changes were overdue.

A man appeared out of the darkness.

He was on the corner down the street, the man in the suit. Leo stepped on his cigarette, watched him approach.

Then he knew what it was that had piqued his interest earlier on: He recognized this guy's walk. The guy was short, slim. Grinning. Somebody he knew.

Then Leo recognized him, and all he wanted to do was turn on his heels and walk away far and fast from this dude who could only mean trouble.

Freddy Robinson came out of the past, extending a hand. "Hey, hey, what up, Lee?"

Leo grasped the hand of his onetime buddy and tried to return a smile. They shook hands, embraced, and stood back to look at each other, and Leo hated to admit it, but it *was* kinda interesting seeing Freddy again, how he looked now. The charmer was still handsome, trim in a sharp suit. "You look great, Freddy."

"Clean living," Freddy spreading his arms, "exercise, fresh air, fruits and vegetables."

"And strong white rum to wash it all down."

Freddy laughed, clapping Leo's shoulder. "You don't look too dusty yourself." He stroked his chin. "What's up with this?"

"Going for the scruffy intellectual look." Leo patted his stomach. "Even started early on the middle-age spread."

Freddy stepped onto the curb beside him. "Still writing the poetry?"

"Yeah, yeah. How 'bout you, still selling auto parts?" Meaning *stolen* parts.

Freddy shook his head, a smile twitching the corners of his lips. "I'm outta parts sales. No money in it. More money in poetry probably."

Leo chuckled, looked away. Guy was still the same. "So what brings you here, Freddy?"

"Had a date. Was in the area, decided to come by and visit you."

Leo pushed his hands in his pockets, trying to appear relaxed. Seven years ago he and Freddy had parted on difficult terms, so Freddy saying he was coming by to visit was heartwarming bullshit. "How did you know I work here, Freddy?"

"Easy, dawg. I just asked around. Contacted people we used to run with back in the day. Ask this one, he tell me to ask that one, that one gave me some info, like that." Freddy gestured to the construction project across the street. "What's that they're building?"

"A new mental health annex. This one behind us here, it's gonna get torn down. Been around since the sixties." Freddy wasn't even listening.

"So how you been keeping, Lee?"

"Fine, fine. So was it my brother told you where I work?"

Freddy angled his head and smirked.

Leo said, "Okay, stupid question."

"Patrick still the same pompous asshole?"

"Careful there, that's my brother you're talking about." Then, "Yeah, of course he is."

"Just so you know, I don't hold anything against him anymore. Or against you. I'm over that. I did some thinking. When I was incarcerated. I had time to reflect and I said to myself, Freddy, dawg, let the past fade. Go out there into the future and seize your opportunity and make something of yourself. So that's what happened. No time for grudges, know what'm saying? I'm through with that, strictly positive vibes I deal with now." Freddy stretched out his fist for a pound.

Leo obliged, self-consciously. Thinking, This guy's got some major balls saying this. But Leo didn't want to delve into all the bad memories, the failed drug deal, Freddy's six-year prison stint. And Patrick, despite his dislike of Freddy, had had nothing to do with any of it. Freddy had gone down because he deserved it, and if not for Patrick's skills as a lawyer, he could've served really serious time, instead of standing here now, spouting self-serving trash. But Leo said, "Glad to hear it. Listen, partner," glancing at his watch, "I've got to run. Can't make a career of this cigarette break." He put out his hand for a shake.

Freddy smiled, ignoring the hand. "I understand. But before you go," and he stepped closer so that he was inches away, "I wonder if you could do a little somethin' for me."

Leo prepared himself for the real reason Freddy had shown up after all these years.

"There's a guy on your floor, an old man, Massani."

Leo watched Freddy look away, acting all nonchalant. "You know him?"

"Not personally. But let's say I *represent* people who do. His former business associates. Mr. Massani is refusing to talk with them, refusing visits from them. There're some matters of grave importance to discuss, so to speak. I was thinking you could be the man to help, you know, arrange a meeting."

Leo said, "Me? I'd like to help but if a patient doesn't want visitors, there's nothing I can do about it, really. We can't force patients out of their rooms to see people they don't want to see. And visitors aren't allowed in patients' rooms, so . . ."

"I hear you, I hear you." Freddy pursed his lips and nodded to show sympathy. "But this is a matter of pressing concern to the people I represent. Whole bunch of them would be affected if this meeting don't happen, feel me? I'm sure you could do *something*." He reached into his inside pocket and produced a roll of cash. He licked his thumb and started counting, flicking the bills. "How much you need, Lee?"

Leo looked away, sighing. "Mr. Massani is in seclusion right now. I don't know if you understand what that is, but he's there under doctor's orders. Patients go in there for different reasons, extreme paranoia or endangering self or staff—" Leo broke off, realizing he was sounding like a policy manual. "Anyhow, once you're there you're not allowed visitors and you don't get out till the doctor signs you out, and he only does that when staff recommends it. So I'm saying, if Mr. Massani didn't want to see visitors before? It's even worse now. Now he *can't*. There's really nothing I can do to help you, honestly."

Freddy shook his head and lifted a finger. "Lemme restate my request." He looked around furtively, stepped closer. "I'm not sure you're comprehending the importance of what I'm asking you, but hey, that's my fault," palming his chest. "Everybody's got something they want to keep private, right? Everybody." He flung an arm out. "Massani. Me. And you. And your brother. Things we want on the down-low. In the dark."

Leo squinted. "What you talking about?"

Freddy said, "Don't play games with me, Lee. You know what I'm talking about."

Fingers of ice swept down Leo's spine, down his legs. He looked at Freddy, slick in his expensive suit, and regretted that two minutes ago he hadn't left this shifty son of a bitch at the curb. He said, "What does that have to do with Massani, Freddy?"

"Everything is related. You should know that, ain't you the poet?" He smirked, returning the roll of cash to his pocket.

"You threatening me, Freddy?"

They were face-to-face now. He could smell Freddy's breath.

Freddy said, "The people I represent would like you to open the door and let Massani out so this meeting can *occur*. Massani is somebody they need, I got a job to do, and I got information concerning a certain incident that you and your brother would prefer be kept secret. This is how important this Massani situation is. You do this for me, for the people I work with, and I'll make sure everything stays under wraps. Provided you help me do my job."

Leo's past had prepared him to expect deviousness from people, so looking at Freddy, he didn't feel shock or disgust, just exhaustion. He thought he was over and done with this shit. His throat tight, not sure if he could speak, he studied the pavement. Finally, he raised his head. "The fact this could cost me my job means nothing to you, huh?" Right away he saw the absurdity of the question. A car drove out of the parking lot and a woman at the wheel waved. Leo waved back, too distracted to notice who it was.

Freddy said, "I'll get back to you on the day and time. This meeting will be at night, of course. This week. Some details still got to be ironed out, but it'll be this week, and since you didn't believe me when I *showed* you," patting his suit pocket, "let me *tell* you. The gentlemen I represent, they'll take care of you, make it worth your while. Tell me if five bills sounds good. Nice little cheddar? Take your woman out for a meal at a fine restaurant, a night in a hotel . . ." He jiggled his eyebrows. Straightened the lapels of his jacket, adjusted his tie. "Got any questions, anything need clarifying?"

Leo shook his head.

Freddy took out a cell phone. "You got a cell?"

"Can't afford it." Leo gazed at him, *through* him.

"What's your number up there on the floor?"

Leo exhaled heavily. "305-555—"

"3097," Freddy said, punching in the last digits. "Just remembered I got it right here." He winked, letting Leo know he already had knowledge. "This ain't no big deal, man. This just plain *bidness.* I got a job to do and you the man with the keys, simple logic. Don't let past disagreements get all tangled up with this. We do this job and afterward we sit down and have a drink, me and you, talk things over. A'ight?" He lifted a hand high with flair, wrist bent, expecting Leo to meet him in a shake.

Leo just watched him before he walked past, brushing the man's shoulder.

"I'll phone with the instructions," Freddy called. "You the dude with the key, Lee. Nod if we on the same page!"

Leo nodded, kept going. Then he heard Freddy, clearly.

"Remember Lonesome Point, Lee."

Leo wheeled around, but Freddy was leaving. Leo watched him walk away under the streetlight, back into the darkness he had come from.

2

FIRST CHANCE HE GOT, Leo flipped through the patients' charts, under the guise of checking Martin's work. Rose was on her break and Martin was in the TV room next door channel-surfing. Leo could hear the news, then sitcom laughter, then a Hummer commercial, while he pored over Herman Massani's chart.

Race: Hispanic. Age: seventy-two. Diagnosis: schizoaffective disorder. Admitting psychiatrist: Dr. Garrido, Rainbow Community Mental Health Center, Hialeah, Florida. Leo had never heard of a Dr. Garrido or a Rainbow Center. He flipped to the Physician's Notes section. Recognized Dr. Burton's chicken scrawl, his signature. Sometimes a doctor counseled another's patient in his absence, so that wasn't out of the ordinary. But why was Garrido so absent? Jefferson Memorial was a public facility, where admitting psychiatrists were also the ones who came two or three times a week to counsel their patients, write orders or scrips. But after the admission pages, there was no evidence of Garrido. Was he on extended vacation? Did he retire? Die? Something about this was odd, and, man, Leo wanted no part of it.

When his break came his head was buzzing. He took a blanket to the staff room, unfolded the bed from the pull-out sofa, and stretched out. Wide awake in the dark. Trying to turn his thoughts toward the life he was creating with Tessa. He thought,

Damn, Tessa, if only you knew the whole truth about me. Well, not only about me, but also the people who helped make me the fucked-up individual that I am.

He got three minutes' shut-eye tops before the phone rang to signal end of break.

IN THE morning, he paid his last dollar to the parking lot attendant and aimed his car for I-95. Wind rushed in the way he liked it, but it wasn't soothing today. Close to home, the needle read empty, so he pulled into a gas station on 135th Street. If memory served, Tessa had said they had seventy-six bucks in the account to last until payday. He slid his debit card and pumped ten dollars' worth, the old Corolla too unreliable to trust with more.

Leo lived in North Miami, in a one-bedroom apartment near the end of 135th. The neighborhood was slipping but holding on to the peace and quiet that he and Tessa liked, which was why they'd stayed. Plus it had a certain charm: the Cuban bodega there on the corner of 135th and Biscayne where he bought his *café con leche* and tostadas; the old Key West–style town houses over here, and then that straight stretch of road under leafy almond trees that led to the gates of his building. Nothing too pretty, but the area was affordable.

Two years ago, he'd met Tessa at a poetry reading at Tobacco Road, where she bartended. They'd talked, he'd drunk and poured out his soul. Can't hardly get stuff published anymore, he'd said. Can't hardly finish a poem. I guess I shouldn't take myself too seriously. She had said, *I* take you seriously. I'm standing here listening to you, aren't I? He returned the next night, and at closing time they kissed in the parking lot as cars drove by. It was a comfortable beginning. She was looking for someone who was mature, responsible. He fit the bill: The years had mostly tamed his impulsiveness, and he was responsible enough. Now, he realized, her agreeable nature and patience made him never want to leave.

In no mood to brave the elevator, he took the stairs to the fifth floor. He walked down the carpeted hallway and smelled breakfast wafting under the doors, rich black coffee. Heard knives and plates clinking, sounds of the ordinary life denied a graveyard-shift fool like him.

He shucked his shoes and clothes at the door, not wanting Tessa to complain again about the germs he was bringing in from the hospital. The bedroom door was closed, Tessa still sleeping. He drank some orange juice at the kitchen sink, scoped his mail in a basket on the dining table. He sifted through the envelopes. Bills and two rejection letters, one from *Iowa Review*, the other from the *Atlantic*.

Shit, who was he trying to fool, thinking the *Atlantic* would ever give him a shot? It was his best poem in the past year, but now that he read it again it felt too light, trivial even. "The Meaning of Sound," he had called it. Whatever.

Tessa was in bed, eyes open. "Hey, you," she said, voice husky with sleep. She was on her side, Wordsworth curled behind her bent legs. The Jack Russell opened his eyes, saw Leo, went back to sleep.

Leo slipped in behind Tessa, wrapped an arm around her bare stomach. He whispered, "You're so warm and cuddly."

She said, "Mmmmm. Your hands are cold."

He nuzzled the back of her neck. She pressed her rump against him. The dog growled, protesting the disturbance. Leo's palm roamed the swell of her stomach, stopped below her belly button. "How's Arsenio doing this morning?"

"Quiet, probably sleeping. And his name is not Arsenio. And we don't know if it's a boy."

"Okay. How's little Natasha doing?"

Tessa groaned. "No, that won't be the name, either. Are we going to start this again? How was your night?"

"You don't like Natasha?" Leo snuggled closer, pressing against her bed-warm skin. "Your belly feels round like a globe. As though it now holds all the little children of the world."

A moment of silence.

"Are you stoned?"

"I'm just a contemplative guy, and I've been contemplating the cycle of life and shit. I've been thinking, if the baby is born black, I should perform one of those African rituals you see in movies—"

"Born black? You've definitely been smoking outrageously strong shit. You promised me you were gonna quit."

"Listen, I'm gonna raise that naked baby up to the sun and say, 'Your name shall be—' "

"Kunta Kinte!"

Leo laughed. He grabbed the dog and stood up with him, feet astride Tessa. He raised the dog in both hands like he was introducing it to the sun, the dog squirming, not appreciating any of this silliness, Tessa giggling and shrieking he was going to drop the dog, put him down.

Wordsworth managed to escape, leaping off the bed and running out of the room.

Leo resumed the snuggling. "Kunta. What a beautiful name, it's so, it's—"

"Stop." Tessa slapped his leg.

Leo nudged the back of her neck with his nose. "You smell so gooood. . . ."

She went, "Hmmm." Then, after a while, "So, you had a quiet night?"

He lay still a moment, wondering whether he should tell her about Freddy. He rolled over onto his back. "A guy I knew from back home dropped by."

"Really? Do I know him?"

"You wouldn't want to meet this guy." He bounded off the bed. Snagged fresh underwear from the dresser drawer. "He's one of the guys I used to get in trouble with. Long time ago." He started toward the bathroom. "I'm gonna take a shower."

"So . . . how'd your friend's visit go?"

He half turned at the door, shook his head. "He's not a friend, Tessa. Just a guy I used to know."

Head on the pillow, she kept her gaze on him. "You don't want to talk about it, do you?"

He shrugged. "Nothing to talk about. He came by, we shot the breeze. He's still a—I don't know, a slimeball. We used to be—okay, we used to be good friends but we kind of went separate ways. It happens."

She smiled and said in hushed voice-over mode, "A figure from his shadowy past."

He left the door partly open while he brushed his teeth, then showered. Sometimes even the bathroom made him claustrophobic. Tessa never teased him. That's what he found attractive about her: She never judged, gave you space, didn't bombard you with questions. She listened. He knew she understood more than she let on. Because she knew that one day he'd tell her everything, in his own time.

She'd already learned a lot about his family, his wild youth, his father's business. She didn't know about Lonesome Point, but had heard bits about his other troubles when he and Freddy had first hooked up here in Miami. The failed drug deal.

She knew something about the end of that story. He'd left out the beginning and the middle. Freddy telling him about a big-time deal, selling hydroponic pot to University of Miami students. Leo using tuition money to put down sixty percent to pay their supplier. Meeting the middleman a couple of days later, a guy named Ortega, a Cuban with a flashy fake Rolex, rings and gold bracelets. Ortega saying, "These guys, they Cubans like just off the fuckin' boat and don't hardly speak no English, so let me do the talking."

Then, he'd always remember this, they were knocking on that apartment door. A man's voice said come in. They opened the door, the apartment was empty, and a Hispanic man, burly and bearded, stood waiting for them in the middle of a dimly lit room.

"Lee?" Tessa was calling to him now. "I'm having a bagel and some fruit, want anything?"

He turned off the shower, stood there dripping wet. "Just some milk, maybe? And a slice of toast, that'd be good."

He toweled off, seeing that Hispanic man's bearded face again, that creepy smile that should have warned him: *Turn around. Run.*

He came out of the bathroom shirtless and sat at the table. Tessa gave him a certain look and he said, "Oh, right," and slouched back into the bedroom, returning with a T-shirt on.

Tessa forked chunks of cantaloupe from a bowl into her mouth, reading *The Miami Herald* spread out on the table next to a plate with a bagel and a tub of cream cheese.

Leo buttered his toast, sipped his milk. He set the glass down, glanced at her, and thought of saying something. He took a bite of toast instead. After he swallowed, he said, "What're you doing today?"

She didn't look up. "I'm gonna go to Wimauma, to the house. Spend the night, come back early tomorrow. I thought I'd clean up some, see what stuff the house needs, what I need to bring the next time."

She'd inherited the farmhouse from an aunt who died last year. It wasn't worth much, but it was hers, theirs, a place they could retreat to.

He said, "I don't want you to work too hard if you're going to do any cleaning. You've cut back your hours at the bar already, so no need to pick up the slack."

"I shouldn't have that much to do. The house was pretty clean last time I saw it."

"The baby. I'd hate to think— You're, what, five months now?"

She put the paper down and smiled at him. "Twenty-one weeks. Aunt Bertha kept that old house in tight shape, Lee. It's just some dusting I might have to do, maybe sweep."

"Promise me no painting, no touch-ups or anything. I read somewhere it's not good for the fetus. Something in the fumes, the lead, I think."

"I promise. And promise me maybe you'll take an extra day off so we can go there next weekend? It's so nice and peaceful up there."

"Oh, yes, so peace—" He dropped his chin and started snoring. She pinched his arm. He enjoyed teasing her about the place, a three-and-a-half-hour drive north, an old two-story wood-frame on two acres in the boonies. Wind ruffling the grass, a sagging wire fence, a dirt road that ran past it.

He looked at her chewing her bagel and said, "That guy that visited me this morning, he's from Belize, his name is Freddy Robinson, I've known him since I was twelve. He was the one I told you about long ago, the one who went to prison."

Tessa put down her bagel and wiped her lips with a napkin. She took her time folding it. After that, she watched him. Waiting.

He knew he was going to tell her more. He always did, in fits and starts, a little here and there. Too much at one time would've scared her. He figured this out a while back, so he kept certain personal stories to a minimum, except for times like these when the pressure was too much. And he always felt better afterward.

WHEN LEO saw the burly guy's bearded face, the slow grin, he knew something was up, and maybe that was just cowardice talking, but he had a bad feeling that night.

They walked into the apartment, Ortega leading the way, Freddy's pockets bulky with the cash. It was a generic apartment, wall-to-wall carpet, white walls, but no furniture. Passing the kitchen, Leo flicked a glance there. No dish rack, pots, pans, nothing on the counters. He told himself, Awright, so nobody lives here, that might be better.

The bearded guy had walked to the center of the empty living room and was just standing there. Like his shoes were nailed to the floor. He nodded at them.

Ortega said, *"Hola."*

Blackbeard smiled his smile and said, "Berry glad to see you!" and a door flew open behind them and the place went dark.

Men started hollering, "Police, police, get on the fucking floor, now, do it now!"

Something smacked Leo on the side of his head and he reeled. It hit him again and he went down. Felt a knee hard in his back. Heard Freddy cussing and fighting with somebody but Leo couldn't see shit. It felt like three people were on top of him. He could hear grunts, groans, fists smacking flesh.

Five minutes later, Leo, Freddy and Ortega lay there on the prickly carpet, ankles and wrists roped. Leo's eyes had adjusted to the dark, and he could see window blinds in another room shifting in the breeze, streetlight falling into the apartment. Eventually, Ortega managed to wiggle free and untied them. No one had to say a word. The cash was gone.

About two months later, two months of trying to convince himself that he'd learned a lesson and wasn't going down that road ever again, Leo met Freddy one night at a club in Coconut Grove. They were sitting at the bar drinking beers, people-watching, when Freddy nudged him.

"Check out the bar across the dance floor. Guy in the flowery shirt, don't he look like that Cuban with the beard?"

Leo stood up and looked. The lighting was bad. It was hard to tell, but Leo thought this guy seemed slimmer.

Freddy said, "Yeah, I think you're right." He lifted his bottle of Harp to his lips, but brought it down fast. "Mothafuck!"

Leo looked again.

Ortega was sitting next to the man, and it was Blackbeard, all right. The two of them yukking it up. Like old buddies.

Freddy sprang up, holding the bottle by the neck like a club, and pushed through the dancers on the floor. Leo shouted after him, "Hold on, now," but Freddy shook him off. Ortega and the Cuban saw Freddy advancing and jumped up and hustled through a side entrance. Leo followed Freddy, saying, "Yo, Fred, forget this, man, let's go, forget this."

He really didn't want to follow, didn't want to be pulled into the violence he knew was coming. But after a minute, he said, "Faawk," and ran after Freddy.

When Leo found him in the parking lot, Freddy had gotten a tire iron from his car and was laying into Ortega and the Cuban. Ortega was no fighter; he cowered against a car, trying to ward off the blows. But the Cuban, face bloodied, was waving a small pistol.

Freddy moved too fast for him. The tire iron was a blur.

For months afterward, everything to Leo was a blur. But he did remember clearly the day in court when the prosecutor asked Freddy why did he pursue Mr. Ortega and Mr. Suarez out of the club. And Freddy saying, "I thought they were old friends I'd recognized." The prosecutor saying, "And is that how you ordinarily greet your old friends, with a tire iron?" Somebody in the courtroom laughing out loud then.

Then it was Leo's turn to testify. He told the truth. That he saw a gun. Patrick was the defense attorney. He worked the self-defense angle hard. He did his best; Leo had to give him that. But the jury was faced with the fact that Ortega, sitting over there at the prosecutor's table looking mopey, had been in a coma for four days and now had a speech impediment. They showed Freddy little sympathy and sent him down for eight years.

Leo drove up to the prison in Starke to visit him a few times. On one visit, Freddy said that Patrick owed him an apology. Leo wanted to know why. Freddy said, "He screwed me good. I put my faith in somebody more concerned about their political career than a black man like me. Tell him this for me. He's an egotistical, incompetent fuck. And I don't want you coming back here, Leo. Better I don't see your face to remind me."

Leo never returned to visit him.

TESSA REACHED across the table to hold his hand. He was glad she knew the full story now so he wouldn't have to feel sneaky about it anymore.

"So that's who Freddy Robinson is." Meaning she had pieced together this version with the condensed version from months back. "You must've been terrified going through all that."

"Scared shitless. Over the period of a few months? I lost like fifteen pounds."

"How long was Freddy in there?"

"Six years. He had two priors, marijuana possession and grand theft. He's damned lucky, he could've been dealt worse, but he doesn't see things that way." Leo shook his head. "Freddy. With him, it's always somebody else's fault, somebody keeping him down."

Tessa said, "What did he want, last night?"

Leo twisted in his seat, released her hand. This was where he had to hold back. A part of the truth was fine but some matters were best contained. "Just came to shout me up. Be a pain in my ass. Show me what a great success he is, wearing this expensive suit, you know? Probably—no, in fact most certainly still keeping up his criminal ways."

Tessa nodded, watching him.

He had to avert his eyes. He didn't care too much whether she believed everything right now; he just wasn't ready to talk anymore.

While she cleaned the apartment, he brushed his teeth again and closed the bedroom blinds and crawled under the sheets.

Dozing off, he could hear her loading the dishwasher, opening and closing closets, the air-conditioning clicking on. He sank into cool slumber, thinking everything was going to be okay, he had to see Patrick today but it was going to be fine, he just needed some sleep.

His eyes snapped open.

He had to see Patrick today. About Lonesome Point.

He stared at the murky ceiling, knowing damn well an already bad day was about to get worse.

3

SIX O'CLOCK THAT EVENING, Leo drove over the Ricken-backer Causeway to Key Biscayne, where his brother lived. He'd called Patrick's office and left two messages with his secretary but hadn't heard back. He had Patrick's cell number somewhere but couldn't find it. Finally, after four, Patrick called back and said he'd been tied up all day in a commission meeting about the airport renewal project, and what could he do for him?

That's how Patrick was, businesslike, no warmth even with his only brother. Leo said he needed to speak to him, in private. When Patrick kept asking about what, Leo said the two words: Lonesome Point.

Patrick fell silent. After a while he said why didn't Leo come to the house this evening, it would be better to speak there, and the kids were asking about him, they hadn't seen him in a long time. Leo wanted to go anywhere but there, but he agreed. After all, Patrick's two kids were sweet, despite their father.

Before Leo left, he realized Tessa had thrown his pants with the roach from last night in the wash. He pulled his stash from the shoe box under the bed and rolled a pinner in his Tessa-free apartment. He fired it standing on the toilet, blowing the smoke into the air vent. Wordsworth the dog came in and observed him. Leo glimpsed himself in the mirror and thought, Christ, he'd been doing this since he was, what, fifteen? Sneaking tokes, having to hide the smell from one person or the other, it was getting pathetic. He'd have to quit.

Eventually.

He was less stressed sitting on the living room sofa, gazing through the window as he put on his shoes and socks, thinking about Freddy. The man who knew too much. Leo had long thought about him that way.

He drove slowly over the Rickenbacker, savoring the rhythm of the buzz, delaying having to see his brother. Either because he was stoned or because he hadn't visited Patrick's in so long, he cruised right past the house and had to U-turn.

It was a quiet street, mostly huge homes, towering hedges, and lots of trees in vast green yards, the kinds that called for gardeners. He drove up Patrick's brick-paved driveway to tall wrought-iron gates, an intercom box on his left. He took a breath and let his head fall back on the headrest.

Six months? Longer? Yeah, longer. He hadn't visited in almost a year. Shameful. Their mother would've never imagined her sons acting this way. But who was responsible for that?

Leo sat up straight and stared at the intercom a full ten seconds before he punched the call button.

Patrick's voice: "Hey, Lee, is that you? Come on in," and the gate swung back slowly.

Leo rolled up the circular driveway past rows of royal palms on either side, a sprawling manicured lawn that sloped down to a seawall and Biscayne Bay. The house with its barrel-tile roof loomed high, casting shade over a section of driveway, the three garage doors, and Patrick's black Porsche Carrera parked there, shiny like a trophy.

Leo walked along cobblestones that curved through hibiscus hedges around to the front, and the waters of the bay came into view across the lawn. He trotted up wide stone stairs, the tall front door opening before he reached it and Patrick still in work shirt and tie standing there to greet him, a hand out.

"Leo, come on in," one hand gripping Leo's, the other touching his shoulder. "You're looking good. Put on a little weight?"

Leo walked into the house, which was always impeccable down to the caramel bamboo floor. "What do they call it? Sympathetic weight gain, something like that? Tessa puts on a pound, I put on a pound," Leo waiting for Patrick to lead the way, the house with its high ceiling and dark wood furniture and plush rugs, Everglades paintings on the walls.

Patrick said, "How's she doing?" touching his stomach, lean from those downtown club exercises.

"No morning sickness. She's lucky. Though I have some nausea now and again when I think about changing diapers."

Patrick grinned, beckoned to him with a tilt of the head toward the living room. They walked through the house, floor-to-ceiling tinted windows overlooking the bay, passed the kitchen, granite countertops, Sub-Zero fridge, glass and maple cabinets. A kitchen like that, Tessa would love. Leo heard movement behind him. He prepared himself, then he turned.

Celina said, "Hi, Leo."

Leo nodded. "Hey, how's it going?"

Celina, his old girlfriend and Patrick's wife the last nine years;

sometimes Leo still could not believe it. Celina, still shapely and petite, black hair as thick and shimmery as it was on the night of the prom.

Patrick said, "Hon, we have any beer? Can I get you a beer, Leo?"

"Water's fine," and Patrick frowned, so Leo said, "Unless you're having . . ."

"Scotch for me. But you're a beer man, I'll get you a brew. We have, Cel?"

Celina nodded. "In the fridge, at the bottom."

Patrick crossed over to the kitchen and Leo and Celina stood looking at each other. Celina broke the tension. "So. How's . . . how's . . ."

"Tessa."

"Yes. Sorry. How's Tessa?"

"Fine. And I'm pretty good myself."

"Of course. You gained weight?"

What was it with these people?

She said, "No, no, it looks good on you. You needed a few pounds. Um, so, you know if it's a boy or girl yet?"

"Next ultrasound. She says she doesn't want to know, but I do. Don't care if it's a boy or girl—"

"As long as it's healthy," Patrick said, returning with a bottle of Beck's and a highball glass of scotch. "I felt the same way with Ethan and Cassie, isn't that so, Cel?" He handed Leo the beer.

Celina said, "Tell Tessa I said hi. I might come by and see her if that's okay? I liked her, that time we met. I think she's great, Leo."

He said, "Yeah? Thanks," and turned around, giving her smile his back. Her performance had been Oscar-worthy.

Out on the terrace, Patrick slumped into a basket-weave chair. Leo waved down to the kids in the pool. "Hey, guys."

Ethan, the younger one, was doing backflips off the diving board; Cassie was sunning her long limbs in a bikini, impersonating a teenager. She shouted up, Uncle Leo, Uncle Leo, saying she was coming up to see him, but Patrick told her to give them a minute, he and Uncle Leo needed to talk.

Ethan kept saying, Uncle Leo, look, watch this one, as he executed another splayed-legs backflip.

Leo took a swallow of beer and sat down in a chair next to Patrick.

Patrick looked over the bay. "So what's going on, Leo?"

"Freddy came by to see me."

"Robinson?"

Leo said the very.

Patrick rubbed his eyes with thumb and forefinger and shook his head. "I figured it would be somebody like that ass to start something. What did he want?"

Leo told him about the visit. Patrick steepled his fingers under his chin, jaw working. Afterward he drank some whiskey and tapped the rim of his glass. "Freddy told you specifically that he would inform the authorities about what happened at Lonesome Point?"

"He didn't say that exactly. He said—well, come to think of it he didn't say who he was gonna tell specifically. He *implied*. Made it sound like if I didn't let them have their little talk with this guy, Herman Massani, I wouldn't be happy about the consequences. Talking about the people he represents, he kept saying that: The people I represent want this to happen."

"I'm asking because who is he going to tell? Somebody with a rap sheet like his, who'd believe him? And that was so long ago. And it didn't even happen in this country. It's crazy."

"So you're saying I should tell him go screw himself?"

Patrick set his drink on the ground and stood up, walked over to the railing. He hitched up his pants, pulled his shoulders straight, the trial lawyer now, eyes on the causeway across the bay. "I saw him once, about a year ago, did I tell you?"

Leo said no, thinking, You and I hardly talk, Patrick, of course you didn't tell me.

"At the airport, I believe it was, he'd just gotten out of prison. Apparently he was still pissed at me for not attending his cousin's funeral, dropping little hints here and there, you know how he does it."

"Sounds like him."

"Talked about how Fonso suffered, the family could hardly pay for the funeral, et cetera?" Leo nodded, and Patrick said, "Cancer is a terrible thing but he shouldn't blame us for it. Fonso was a good guy, no one would wish that on him."

Leo waited to see where this was leading. He didn't know how to handle this situation. He realized he was hoping Patrick would help, maybe give him the word: Yes, go ahead, let him out. Or: Tell Freddy to go to hell.

Patrick was saying, "Freddy is an ingrate. He could still be behind bars. He was very fortunate I agreed to defend him, I should remind him. He could've been stuck with a public defender and where would he've been? Doing ten to twelve in Florida State, that asshole." Patrick turned around, leaned back against the railing. He inhaled deeply, shoved his hands in his pockets. "If there's anything I learned . . . ," shaking his head. "You know I built my career, built everything I have through hard work, sure, but through preparation, too, mainly preparation is what I'm talking about. Anticipate some event, then prepare for it." He returned to his seat, this time dropping elbows on knees, leaning close. "Two months ago one of my secretaries was causing some trouble, I suspected where it might end up so I sat her down, we had a chat, found out she wanted severance. We signed off on a little agreement, now that matter is settled. What was happening, she was making noises about my campaign, accusing it of improprieties, who knows what else. If I hadn't talked to her? God knows what else she would've cooked up. With Freddy, now, it might be a little different. I expected something like this could happen but I still have to be careful, *extra* careful now. Now it matters to me more because I'm not just another Joe Blow, I'm a county commissioner, Lee, I have much more to lose. It's a bigger pot. I've worked too hard for my career, my family, my kids. See where I'm going with this?"

"You're saying go ahead and let the man out."

"I'm not saying that at all. What if this is a shakedown? Or what if Freddy comes back with some other demand? I'm not prepared to give that piece of shit any control over me. Do you understand the complexity of this, Leo?"

"I'm not an idiot, Patrick."

"Look. We give Freddy what he wants, maybe he goes back

under the rock he came from. Or we bend to him now and watch him come back and then watch us keep on bending."

Leo shrugged. "So then . . ."

Patrick sipped his drink. "So we do nothing." He looked directly at Leo. "Understand? Nothing. We wait."

"And if he comes back?"

"Then we *burn* that bridge when we come to it."

Leo thought that sounded so fucking easy. He took a swig of beer, rubbed his eyes, already tired of this conversation. "If I let this man out, they discover it was me, I might be out of a job. I just want you to know that."

Patrick straightened. "Don't worry about this. Come on, Lee. Am I your brother or am I your brother? If it ever comes to that, I'll take care of you. Till you find something else."

Leo thought of saying, That's what I'm afraid of. But he held back, sucked on the beer.

Patrick said, "What's on your mind?"

"I don't know." Leo pinched the bridge of his nose. "Aren't you tired of this?"

Patrick leaned back and looked at him. "Of what?"

"You know what. It's like a ghost. Chasing us. We can't seem to shake it."

"Leo."

"Always around the corner, something else nasty or looking to threaten your happiness. All this fallout from Dad's business, like it won't go away, it can't just fucking lay down and *die*."

"Leo, cut it out."

"I'm telling you, Patrick, believe me, the old man messed us up good."

"Quit it, you hear me?" Patrick's voice rising as the French doors behind them opened and Celina popped her head out.

They all looked at each other in silence.

Celina said, "Leo, you staying for dinner?"

Leo gave it a moment, for manners. "Thanks, but, uh, I got to be someplace in a little bit. Thanks, though."

Celina said to Patrick, "We're having pork chops, sautéed baby bella mushrooms, and steamed broccoli. What kind of wine?"

"The Shiraz would be perfect."

Celina said okay and glanced at Leo before she closed the door, or maybe Leo only imagined the glance.

Patrick said, "I understand you're worried. How do you think I must feel? I feel like I'm at risk. I say let's keep our heads and we'll get through this fine."

Leo was having difficulty with the "How do you think I must feel?" Whenever he talked to Patrick too long he felt tension knotting his throat, like now. He decided it was time to leave.

Patrick said, "You're gonna say hi to the kids?"

Leo said sure he would and felt guilty for hoping Patrick would forget. They walked around the terrace to the back stairs, getting another view of the bay.

It was sweet the way Patrick lived, in his little piece of paradise, a beautiful wife, two good-looking kids, a Porsche out front. Leo was envious: There, he admitted it. While Patrick had climbed the status ladder, Leo had gotten serious and practiced the habit of following rules, working hard, and if honest employment meant living one step up from poverty, so be it.

Maybe it was better than having political ambitions and a crick in your neck from forever looking over your shoulder.

"Uncle Leo!" Cassie screamed and came running, arms wide for a hug.

Holding her aloft by her thin hips, Leo whirled her around, and felt himself hoping for a daughter just like her.

4

DUSK HAD SETTLED while Patrick sat with his second scotch and soda by the pool. He leaned back and spat out an ice cube high, watching it arc down into the water with a plop.

A door opened on the terrace and Celina appeared in the shaft of light from the house. She sashayed over to the railing. "How long will you be down there, Mr. Worrywart?"

He raised his drink. "I'll be up in two sips."

"Ethan needs help with his geometry. Which one's an isosceles triangle again, I forget."

"Tell him I'll come up in a sec to explain. Hey, give me a moment, will you, Cel?"

Celina pursed her lips, tapping the railing. "Sure." Spinning around and stalking back inside.

When he went up he'd be in for a frosty few minutes. Then she'd probably launch into one of her we-don't-spend-any-time-together harangues and he'd have to sit down and reassure and talk softly and promise he'd knock off early one day this week, Friday maybe, they'd go to Joe's Stone Crab just the two of them, leave the kids with the babysitter.

Jesus, marriage was exhausting sometimes. Some days he wanted to tell her, You don't know how good you've got it. Never worked hard a day in her adult life. Everything she ever wanted, more money in her weekly allowance than some of his firm's secretaries took home in a month, she needed to quit whining.

But he'd never dare say any of that because that would mean a huge fight and she'd only retort like she did once: Oh, and I have you to thank for all this happiness? Don't you ever forget who has been behind you all these years, you didn't make it all on your own, sir.

She was right. Through all his major challenges—law school, his first year of private practice, his first political race—she'd been his rock. The woman was strong-willed, but difficult sometimes. She'd never forgiven him for the fact that he grew up with money and she didn't, had always needed to work summer jobs as a teenager while he caroused, his father being . . . Well, whatever Ivan Varela had been, he was wealthy. But when did Patrick ever brag about that?

She'd say it wasn't what he said, it was how he acted. And how was that? With this freaking, insufferable sense of entitlement, she'd say. As if somehow he'd achieved everything by his hard work and intelligence and not because he'd been lucky enough to be born into the right family and lucky enough to marry a woman like her. Modesty wasn't one of Celina's traits.

Then they'd get into this whole am-I-a-good-spouse argument that always led nowhere. Hell, he *was* a good husband. Tried to be, every single day. At least he wasn't like Leo, who did everything to avoid responsibilities like marriage and a career, including remaining a teenager deep into his twenties. Look where that got him. Working a menial job, living hand to mouth at age thirty-two. What kind of father was he going to make?

Leo had caused their parents enough grief to last two generations. Suspended from high school twice; arrested for marijuana possession back in Belize; dropped out of college; then his testifying about that assault on the drug dealers, which Patrick had never divulged to their parents. Leo's inability to stay under the radar had been a disappointment to the old man, who had built a lucrative under-the-table business over several years without a hint of a criminal record.

As for himself—Patrick thought he was a good father: attentive, affectionate, like their father had been before business consumed his life. And Patrick was certainly a better husband. Patrick had never cheated on Celina.

And Leo? Had he ever been faithful to anyone he dated before breaking their hearts? His fiancée had a disappointing marriage ahead, only she didn't know that yet. Patrick was positive that Celina, way back, had sensed that Leo would amount to nothing, which was why she had ended it with him. For crying out loud, the man wasn't even faithful to himself because he hardly knew himself, he was a moving target.

Patrick rose with his cell phone and walked away from the pool and the house, toward the seawall. The lights of downtown Miami high-rises glinted from across the water. They said to him: Enjoy the view, but keep your distance. Admire the beauty, but remain clean. So far he was listening. Trying real hard to keep his name unsullied. He scrolled through the numbers on the cell and found the one he needed.

He glanced back at the house, lights on in the living room, kitchen, kids' rooms. Cassie probably lying on her side in bed yapping on the phone, schoolbooks she hadn't cracked strewn amid magazines like *Seventeen* and *CosmoGirl*. Ethan probably doodling in his notebook, trying to avoid deciphering math problems on his own, preferring to wait for Patrick to explain.

It struck Patrick, as it had before, standing there about to make a private phone call, that maybe he was more like his father than he was willing to admit. Ivan Varela would sometimes disappear down in the yard to discuss business. This was back in the eighties, early nineties, and he'd take out one of those old brick-looking analog cell phones and talk standing by the fence, admiring the view of the harbor.

But no, Patrick was decidedly *not* like his father. He'd discovered that years ago.

5

PATRICK MADE THE BIGGEST DISCOVERY of his life when he was twenty, back home from college on spring break. He walked into the kitchen one morning and saw his mother stirring cake batter, crying quietly. She was not an emotional woman, so this alarmed him. He asked her what was the matter.

She wouldn't say, averting her eyes and telling him to just leave her be a minute.

He hovered, knowing it had to be something about Leo. What had he done this time? Her mother said it wasn't him. Patrick refused to leave the room, he and his mother had this bond.

"It's your father," she finally said to him.

"Is he okay? Did something happen?"

She poured the cake mix into a pan. She tilted the pan to level the mix. Put the mixing bowl into the sink. Wiped her hands on a dish towel.

"Mom?"

"He's okay. He may have lost his mind, but he's okay."

Patrick didn't know what to say. He'd never seen his mother acting so weird. He watched her turn on the oven to preheat. He moved out of the way when she said excuse me, please, and reached around him for the sponge by the sink. She started washing the mixing bowl, her back to him.

"Mom. Please tell me what's going on."

"It doesn't concern you, Patrick. It's your father I should be talking to, not you."

"Mom, I'm twenty years old. I think I deserve to know when I see you behaving like this. What did Dad do?"

She finished washing, stacked the bowl in the dish rack. She put the cake in the oven, turned on the timer, and sponged the countertops clean. Patrick simply refused to leave the room. When she started talking, she was still bustling about the kitchen: folding dish towels, pulling a chicken out of the freezer to thaw in the sink. "Your father has a very short memory, it appears."

"Explain, please."

"I will say about as much as I need to. This is still a matter for him and me, so don't *explain please* me. Now, if I'm not happy at the moment, it's because I sense that my home is threatened. Your father has lost sight of what makes us a family. He's doing things that are highly upsetting. He knows there're some people who resent his standing and what he's achieved with his business, so you'd expect him to be more prudent. But another thing he's lost is his respect for this family, it seems that way to me, and should he continue, oh, I pray and hope he doesn't lose us."

"Mom, I don't under—"

"Shh. Your father, Patrick, is a loving, fine man who has deep flaws. No different from lots of people. But he's also a man of certain appetites that I can't satisfy and I'll never be able to." She rearranged pots in a high cabinet with a clatter. "I'm not saying any more about this. But I want you to know, I've never felt . . ." Her eyes welled up. "I've never felt so alone in my marriage." She turned to the sink and poured water over the frozen chicken. "What's been happening has been going on for a while.

It's becoming disrespectful and I won't put up with it, I simply won't. But it's between him and me, it's something we'll do our best to resolve. I'm being honest with you, dear. You saw me upset, so I'm telling you this, but I won't say any more for the time being."

Patrick kissed his mother on the neck and walked out of the room. He sat on the front steps and wondered awhile before he got up and walked to his friend Fonso's house.

IT WAS around six P.M., a Friday. People were getting off work, driving faster than usual, streets crowded.

Workmen waited at the bus stop at the beginning of the Northern for the bus to take them home to the districts. Bicyclists flowed into the spaces between cars and pedestrians.

Patrick headed up the Northern in Fonso's old pickup. He pulled into the parking lot of a dingy Chinese restaurant across the road from his father's place. He parked behind an SUV so that he was partially hidden but could still see the glass building, lights on in his father's third-floor corner office. The BMW was parked in the front lot behind closed gates.

Patrick bought a Fanta from the restaurant and drank it in the truck as night came on. Around seven-thirty, the office lights went out, and some minutes later his father emerged from the building, briefcase in hand.

Patrick followed the BMW into the city, staying well back, allowing a car or two to get between them. He tried to keep his mind blank. Not wishing for any unpleasant revelation yet expecting it, even more so when his father turned right at the roundabout instead of circling around toward home.

Where was he going? Patrick didn't know of any business dealings his father had in southside Belize City.

They drove over the Belcan Bridge and down Central American Boulevard, the uneven road jostling Patrick. His father turned right onto a narrow street, entering a rough area that Patrick usually avoided and where—as far as he knew—none of his father's business associates lived. Workers, maybe, but not associates. His father hung another right, a narrow dirt street that ran past stilt houses in yards choked with weeds, shanty shops here and there, tires and other debris streetside. Patrick maintained a fifty-yard distance from the BMW. There were only a few other cars on the street, everybody creeping around the potholes.

Another right, past shacks and empty lots, and Patrick was lost.

The dirt road stretched ahead in the night. Only he and his father on the road, dust billowing on both sides. Patrick focused on the taillights.

When the brake lights flashed, he inhaled deeply and his mind started spinning.

How did he know he was about to see something he didn't want to, that would change his life? He just knew. This was a knot in his heart that needed to be untangled.

He parked far away from the concrete, tin-roofed house where his father had stopped. He watched him get out of the car, open a wrought-iron gate, and enter the yard. In the driveway was a car Patrick recognized, the Reverend's silver Jaguar. But this wasn't the Reverend's house.

Patrick stepped out onto the road, darkness all around, toads bleating in the bushes. There were no other homes nearby and a single streetlight shone where the road dead-ended up ahead.

He watched his father climb the stairs. The front porch light was on. A screen door opened and a young man Patrick had never seen before greeted his father. The young man put a hand on his father's arm, they embraced. They went inside, the screen door slapped shut, and a wooden door closed after that.

Patrick sat in the car with the windows down. Music and men's laughter filtered into the street. Lights in one part of the house blinked off, and a light in a bedroom window came on.

Five minutes later, the bedroom lights were out, the entire house in darkness, with Patrick watching it, alone with his fears.

6

CELL PHONE IN HAND, Patrick gazed at the lights of the downtown high-rises. No way was he like his father. He knew how to separate business from pleasure. How to detect false friends. When it was time to cut someone from your life. Where to find information so as to prevent rude surprises. He dialed and put the cell phone to his ear.

The old Cuban's voice came on the line. "Good evening, Patrick."

"*Cómo estás, Oscar?*"

"Very fine, considering the alternatives."

"I'd like to discuss something that I found out this evening. Have a minute?"

Oscar said he did. Then, "But what kind of business is it?"

Patrick cleared his throat. "It's that kind of business."

"I thought as much. Give me a second, I'll call you back."

A minute later, Patrick's cell chirped.

Oscar said, "Sorry, but one can never be too cautious. What can I do for you this evening, my friend? I'm staring at a Bolívar on my desk that's begging me to wrap my lips around her, so please let's make this quick, or failing that, interesting; you think you'll do that?"

"A fellow by the name of Freddy Robinson paid my brother a visit yesterday at his work, Jefferson Memorial psych ward. It concerns a patient there. Somebody wants him out, wants my brother to let him out. If not, they, whoever these people are, are threatening to spill something about my past in Belize. Which I can't go into right now, but that's the situation. Needless to say, I'm troubled by this and I can't just let it lie. I need to know what's going on, who's behind this. What I need, actually, is for Freddy Robinson to go away."

Oscar breathed heavily into the phone. Patrick could picture him in his home office, the dark cherrywood chair and desk, a crystal ashtray, cigar cutter, and humidor on the desk next to a stack of manila folders of "paperwork"—Oscar's name for it— of his diverse dealings with businessmen and politicos, detailed reports of meetings and conversations, all of it a record of his as- sociation with Miami's movers and shakers and would-be lead- ers. Patrick heard the click of the lighter and lip-smacking as Oscar fired up the Bolívar.

After a slow exhale, Oscar said, "Freddy Robinson. Where have I heard that name before?"

"He's the guy from Belize who I defended years ago, an ag- gravated battery case. He went to prison. Before that he worked off and on for our mutual friend, the late Alejandro Parra."

"Oh? I don't remember him."

"You remember the Hialeah car-dumping scandal? Involved about a couple dozen cars bought from Parra's son's dealership. They were reported stolen and the owners all received insur- ance claim payments. But what investigators came to find out, young Bobby Parra was in money trouble so had hired this fel- low, Freddy Robinson, to strip the cars, sell the parts to salvage yards, and Bobby, Freddy Robinson and the car owners split all the money from the insurance and car parts. You remember that?"

"Ah, yes, it's coming to me. A stupid little business. But nobody was convicted for it, if I recall. So this Robinson is something of a small-timer?"

"That he is. But now he's working for somebody else. Can't be Bobby Parra because he's in prison for racketeering. I hate to bother you about this, but I thought you might know, seeing as how Robinson once worked for Alejandro." Patrick could hear Oscar sucking on the cigar.

"You hate to bother me? Don't lie. You relish it because you're a nervous man and you know I'll calm your troubled mind. Too bad you can't trust me enough to tell me the nature of this bad news that Robinson claims to know about you."

"Did I say it was bad news, Oscar? I didn't say that."

"No, no. What you said, you used the word 'spill.' As in spill the beans. Or spill blood. You can't discuss this thing in your past right now?"

"Certainly not over the phone."

"When you came to me years ago, you said you wanted to win the Cuban vote and even though you're not a Cuban running in a heavily Cuban district, we worked together, and what happened? Tell me."

"We won, Oscar. I'm the first non-Cuban county commissioner my district has ever seen. I'm in your debt."

"Yes, we won, and now it's the mayoral race and we're off to another great start. Why? Because we trust each other. In order for me to help, I need to know you keep trusting me and I need to know this isn't something that will wreck our campaign. We must talk, *mi amigo*, sooner or later. I have too much invested in you. I've gotta be adamant about this."

"We'll talk, Oscar. I promise. But right now I need you to do two things for me."

Oscar was silent.

Patrick wondered if he'd sounded too impatient. He'd never been skilled at ass-kissing.

"How can I help you, *mi amigo*?"

"Can you talk to the Parra family? Ask if Freddy Robinson is working for one of them?"

"And the second thing?"

Patrick took a moment. "Herman Massani. Ask the Parras who he is. That's what I need to know. Who the hell is Herman Massani?"

7

LEO OVERSLEPT, then his car wouldn't start and he had to race upstairs to beg a neighbor for a jump. He was running fifteen minutes late, no fuel in his system except a glass of milk and a side of stress adrenaline. Fortunately, I-95 wasn't too crazy that time of night, but he had to wait two years at a red light on Twelfth Avenue.

Once at work, he rushed up the stairs, clipping on his badge. By the time he stepped onto the floor of Annex 3, the change-of-shift meeting in the conference room was winding down, and Rose cut her eyes at him when he skulked in, slid into a seat.

The night didn't improve when they informed him the three-to-eleven shift had received a late admission and had no time to sort through the patient's belongings, so he'd have to do it. And don't forget to make more patients' charts, nurses were running low, and also, please, get Cenovia Delgado ready for a seven A.M. CAT scan, got that, Leo?

Yeah, you're welcome. He knew why they "had no time" to sort through the patient's clothes. Because they reeked and were caked with all manner of filth, which wasn't unusual, but this patient's garments were probably packing enough of a stench that they pawned the job off on the eleven-to-seven shift.

Later, pulling on the gloves, Leo said, "Hey, Martin, lemme

show you the procedure for checking in patients' belongings," and motioned for Martin to follow him.

But Rose said no, she wanted Martin to get more practice filling in the charts. "Sit here, I want to show you something," patting the chair next to her in front of the computer. "You know how to schedule appointments? No? Quick little lesson, then."

Martin shrugged at Leo and sat in the chair.

Leo shook his head and walked out of the nurses' station and down the hall. A few patients were up and about, two in the TV room, one weighing himself on the scale in the dining room. Leo opened the laundry room with one of his keys, found the drawstring plastic bag of clothes on a shelf above the washer. On the bag was a label with the patient's name: Reynaldo Rivera. The guy police had brought into Crisis the night before, the spitter.

Leo was right about the clothes, sewer quality. Mud-caked jeans. Pissy underwear. Man, did he need this job that much? The actual shit he had to endure. He put the washer cycle on heavy soil, dumped in a half cup of Surf, and hustled out of the room for a gulp of air. Goddamn, the whole unit stank, pine oil hardly masking the urine. On the way to the kitchen for a cup of cold water, he saw Frankie Reyes sitting in the TV room with a hand down the front of his pajamas. Leo popped his head around the door. "Yo, cut that out."

Frankie looked up at him all dreamy. He drew his hand out slowly and crossed his legs.

Frankie was at it again when Leo returned from the kitchen. Leo said, "Maaaan . . ."

Frankie said, "I ain't never had none, that's why. I ain't *never* had none. I ain't never had *none.*"

"Why don't you go to your room anyway? It's time for me to lock up."

Frankie shuffled out holding up his pants by the front. "See you later, Leo. Hey, shoot some hoops down in the courtyard with me one night?"

"Maybe we can do that when you get discharged, all right?"

Frankie put out his hand for a shake.

Leo looked at the hand and patted him on the shoulder. "Night, Frankie."

When Leo walked back into the nurses' station, Rose's palm was on Martin's back, their heads close together at the computer monitor. Leo stood quietly a few seconds; they didn't even know he was there. Rose's fingers were gently kneading Martin's shoulder. Small circular motions with the palm now. Martin sat stiffly.

"Yes, that's it," Rose just about cooed. "Make sure you enter the appointment time before you fill in anything else, and don't forget the admitting floor. I like that cologne. And enter the doctor's name right over there . . . uh-huh." She was kneading his neck now, staring at his profile. "You're so *tense*. Everything's easier when you're relaxed, don't you know?"

Leo was beginning to feel embarrassed. Not that he didn't want to see how far this would go, but he needed to act professional here. He tried. For two seconds. Then he said in a booming voice, "Anyway, so as I was thinking," and walked toward them, and Martin jumped, while Rose removed her hand from his neck and coolly turned around. "Something the matter?"

A smile tickled Leo's lips. "No, I was just, you know, thinking."

"Wow, amazing."

"I was thinking maybe we ought to keep Frankie out of the TV room, or get him a private room or something, since he's always abusing himself like that. Guy should have a little privacy."

Rose stared at him. "You know who deserves something? Mr. Massani in SR two needs his urine bottle changed. For some reason, he acted up this afternoon and they put him in two-point restraints. Looked almost like he *wanted* to go into seclusion. But anyway, since you missed just about the entire meeting you should read up on the evening shift's notes, they're over there on the clipboard. When you go to Mr. Massani, take him a cup of apple juice, too, and might as well change his sheets while you're there." She turned back to the computer.

Leo bit his tongue and walked out. One month. He was giving himself one month to find something else. That shouldn't be too hard. Any job would be easier than having to face this busy-work bullshit night after night when he should be home sleeping instead. Yeah, boy, it was time to get serious and move the hell off the psych ward.

He took out his keys, opened the seclusion room door. The stink of piss hit him out of the darkness.

Massani's voice said, "*Quién es?* Who is there, please?"

Leo flipped on the light.

Massani was stretched out on a sheeted plastic mattress, left ankle and right wrist cuffed with thick rubber restraints. A full bottle of urine stood by the bed.

Leo felt sorry for him. Such an old, frail guy, someone's father

or uncle. Then he remembered . . . or probably somebody's
henchman.

Leo said, "Who are you, Herman?" thinking out loud.

The old man said, *"Tengo sed. Un vaso de agua fria, por favor."*

"So you don't speak English?"

"No habla español?"

"No, I don't *hablo* that well. But I think you understand me
fine. We're going to need to change your clothes and your sheets
now, Herman. Afterwards you'll get your *agua fria* or juice or
something."

"Please. Water now? I am very thirsty."

Leo went to the kitchen, filled a Styrofoam cup with ice and
water, and brought it back. Herman pushed up with a hand
and sat up. He took the water, gulped it down, Adam's apple
bobbing. A week's growth of white whiskers running down to
his neck. Pale blue eyes. What kind of character shady enough
to be hunted by Freddy Robinson and his ilk landed in a psych
ward? People like that were sometimes stupid but they weren't
schizo—this guy's chart said he was schizoaffective, even though
there were no antipsychotics prescribed, but Ativan and Prozac,
an antianxiety and an antidepressant. According to the chart,
he'd been in and out of Rainbow Community Mental Health
Center. So surely he didn't have the kind of mind for organized
crime.

If indeed the records told the truth.

Leo changed Herman's pajamas, cleaned the floor with several
towels and a disinfectant spray. Slipped a fresh sheet on the mattress, dumped all the dirty linen in a big plastic bag, and snapped

the restraints back on Herman, right ankle and left wrist this time.

He went off the floor through a side door and down the hall to the laundry chute. He thought about sneaking downstairs for a quick cigarette, but Rose was in superbitch mode tonight and he didn't want to push it. He hauled his ass back onto the floor and into the nurses' station. Nobody there. That was odd; Rose was such a stickler. He wheeled the gerri chair from the dining room out to the hall, threw a sheet over it. Then he got Herman's chart from the cart and kicked back.

Under the three-to-eleven shift's notes section:

> 20:30: Patient showing signs of agitation, banging on glass. Patient refuses to heed staff's instruction and continues to strike glass with hands. Patient paranoid, restless. Claims new male patient wants to harm him.
>
> 21:15: Patient placed in 2-pt. restraints. 2 mg. Ativan administered. Patient apologetic. Denies any intention to harm self. Remains paranoid about other patient wanting to harm him.
>
> 22:50: Patient sleeping.

Leo flipped through other sections of the chart but nothing out of the ordinary jumped out at him.

He heard a door open down the hall and here came Rose and Martin out of the supply closet, Martin carrying a cardboard box. Leo pushed down the footrest and set his feet on the floor, to look more professional.

Passing by, Martin said, "Mouthwash, toothbrushes, and stuff."

Now, why'd he feel the need to announce that?

Rose waltzed by, strands of her black hair loosened from her bun. Leo wondered . . . Nah, that was normal. If a couple of buttons on her dress were undone, or she was perspiring a little, say, then yes, but otherwise, he'd give them the benefit of the doubt.

Rose stopped at the nurses' station's door. "You've got first break, you know that? You should go now."

Leo said all right, he just wanted to write some notes on Massani since he'd already dealt with him tonight. He pulled the pen from his pocket, uncapped it, kept his eyes on the page. Soon as Rose disappeared inside, he flipped to the Personal Information section and found Massani's address of record. He wrote it on an old receipt from his wallet: *252 E. 49th Street, Hialeah.*

In the nurses' station Rose and Martin were talking softly, close to each other while Martin stocked plastic-wrapped toothbrushes and small tubes of Crest in a high cabinet. Leo slipped the chart back in the cart and headed to the staff room, officially on break.

He wondered whether he should tell Martin about Rose, warn him about the shit he was going to step into. But then, he probably wouldn't believe what Leo knew: that the shift head nurse was as off-kilter as the patients.

MORNING RADIO was busy with gasbags and bloviators, no matter the goddamn station he punched. Still chattering about nonsense like Tom Cruise jumping on Oprah's couch and how very secretive and mysterious Scientology was. What was mysterious was how any sensible person could waste time listening to such trifle. Man, he was in a sour mood, and he knew what was bothering him: this Herman Massani situation. His gut telling him something was going to go down and he'd find himself in the middle of it. His chest was tense, his throat a knot. Patrick only had to give him the word and he'd let them have the old man and maybe he'd be able to breathe easy again.

Wasn't like the old man meant anything to him. He'd been there less than a week, didn't speak much; Leo didn't really want to know him.

So why the hell was he driving to 252 East 49th Street, Hialeah? Curiosity. Common sense. You just did not tell a man to risk his job and not expect him to ask the obligatory questions. Such as, *Why?* "Because we could blackmail your politician brother" was not really a satisfactory answer. Maybe the real answer had to do with the question *Who?* As in, who is this man Herman Massani that my shady former friend Freddy Robinson, *representing* certain people, wants off the ward?

Leo didn't like any of the scenarios he was coming up with. He wanted no hand in any criminal scheme, a scheme he suspected would be unhealthy for the old man. He didn't care that Patrick's reputation was on the line. Patrick had always been the supposed upstanding son, the good boy, but Leo would be damned if he'd act on Patrick's say-so before knowing what the real deal was with Massani.

He exited the highway onto 49th and was counting down streets, lowering the music to concentrate, tapping the brake in the morning traffic. Street vendors at one corner hawking plastic bags of limes; at the cross street one guy walking down the center stripe selling churros from a box slung around his neck. One woman in the median under an umbrella selling frosty bottles of water from a red cooler. Horns blared, people yelled to each other in Spanish. Leo slowed for a yellow light and watched a city bus belch exhaust as it ran the red, then braked for two jaywalking girls in plaid Catholic school skirts.

Hialeah always confused the hell out of him. He eased into the right lane, reading the even storefront numbers, counting down. When he saw 260 on a Spanish-style iron fence he knew he was close, so he turned right onto Fourth Avenue and parked in the first empty space streetside, deciding it was easier on foot.

He got out and headed west along the sidewalk, undoing his top shirt buttons in the heat. Right off, he knew something was amiss. There were no homes on his side, the even-numbers side of the street, only doctors' offices and stores and fast-food joints. He found 252, a small office building behind a low concrete fence, no gate. He strolled up the walkway to an iron-grille door. A sign on the door: DR. ALFREDO GARRIDO, M.D., PSYCHIATRY. The door was locked. He rang the bell. After a minute, he walked around to the side of the building, all the frosted glass louvers closed. The place looked abandoned, the grass patchy and brown in spots, pages of a windblown newspaper against the fence. He hit the bell again. He checked his watch—9:05. The good doctor should've been in by now, or at least a receptionist.

Leo headed back to his car, thinking maybe Massani was homeless and the only address the old man knew offhand was his doctor's. Crossing Fourth Avenue to his car, he saw a towering black guy, head perfectly shaved, lumber out of the Cuban bakery on the corner, carrying two steaming Styrofoam cups of coffee. Holding them out, away from his sharp sportcoat, bright blue tie, and natty black slacks, the spiffy clothes and careful grooming probably the reason Leo's attention had swung to him in the first place. Guy reminded him of Freddy, a few threads overdressed for any gritty urban experience. Leo tracked him as he walked to a car three spaces up, a black Mercedes.

Leo stood still when he saw the person in the front passenger seat.

The big man had stopped at the car and was handing one of the cups through the window, and Freddy Robinson reached out and took it. He said something to the big man, who put his cup on the car's roof and crossed Fourth Avenue toward a convenience store.

Leo kept walking, thinking no way this could be a coincidence. But relax, he told himself, relax, this might be a good thing. Maybe Freddy would let him know more now. He walked over to Freddy's side. "Yo, Fred. What you doing around here?"

Freddy finished sipping coffee, put the cup on the dash. "What's up this fine morning, Lee?" Real casual, no surprise to see him. Which made Leo pretty certain they'd spotted him a while ago, maybe even trailed him. If not, they'd been hanging around the doctor's office, waiting. Hunting someone.

Leo gestured to the bakery. "My fiancée, she likes the pastries. Sometimes I stop by, get a few." He watched Freddy reach for his coffee, blow on it, take another sip. Put the cup back on the dash and adjust his yellow necktie. The man looked completely *GQ*, cool blue long sleeves, diamond earrings in both ears.

"*Pastelitos, café con leche*, man, that's some good shit. I'd like me some a that myself, only I got to watch the weight." Freddy touched his stomach. "Yeah, boy. We getting older, Lee. Used to be I could wolf down any ol' greasy-greasy and get away with it. How about you? Still could eat whatever?"

"Not so much anymore."

"Bet you don't even have to run or nothin'."

"Only when people are chasing me."

"You've always been skinny like me, though. But watch this face now." Freddy puffed out his cheeks, patted them. "All this weight I been putting on. One sixty-five now. For somebody my height? Never would a thunk it. High cholesterol, too, the doctor told me the other day. And diabetes runs in my family so I got to watch that, can't eat too much sweets, got to exercise more."

Leo looked off down the street. "Just tell me when. I'm ready whenever you are, awright?"

Freddy reached for his coffee, a trace of a smile on his lips. He said, "Hmmm," and took a slow sip. Put the cup back and straightened his tie before he turned to Leo. "Getting impatient there, partner."

"I just want this over with." Leo twirled a finger by his head. "Been thinking about it constantly and I don't want to do that anymore. I want this thing done. Over." He beat back the urge to say, And I want to be done with you and your slippery ways, not see your face again.

Freddy gazed into the distance. "Patience is a virtue sayeth the Lord." He grinned at Leo. "Or something like that. Who said that anyway? Jesus? Or is that a proverb, like out of the Bible or something? Your brother was here, he'd be correcting me right quick, 'member back in the day? Patrick, Mr. Intellectual?"

Freddy sucked his teeth, brushing something off his pants. "That know-it-all mothafucka." He nodded to himself and scanned Leo head to toe. "Patience, Lee. Things happen when they should happen, not before, and it's when you force it you encounter serious difficulties. I learned that when I was in lockdown."

Leo rubbed his jaw. Here we go again.

"Two years to develop patience, concentration. Poise." He looked hard at Leo. "Probably it was better you didn't get that opportunity like me. Was rough in there, nigger, rough. Constant threat all day. You feel like violence gonna erupt anytime from one corner or the other. Thick tension, dawg. I seen one dude get knifed, rusty-ass shiv, thirty-two times. Disemboweled right in front a me. Nasty sight. To get through this shit day after day, you don't push things. You lie low, feel me? Keep your face serious, stay cool, and do your time, with patience. Now I'm out here, liberated, steady doing my thing and gettin' paid, and I will *not* be rushed. When I see fit to request the go-ahead, then you'll get the green light. But you got to just chill and let me make that decision, know what'm sayin'?"

Leo threw out his hands. "Hey, I'm just saying, I'm ready when you are."

Freddy nodded. "Here come Bernard now," pointing his chin at the big man crossing the street, the big man throwing a look at a car that started slowing way down for him. Freddy said, "Want you to meet him." He shouted through the open driver's window, "Yo, Big B, come this side."

The big man came around, diamonds glinting off several fingers, a thick gold bracelet. He reached out for a shake, grinning boyishly.

Freddy said, "Leo, this is Bernard Brown; Big B, this is Leo Varela, used to be my dawg way back when."

Bernard's hand swallowed Leo's like he was shaking with a goddamn first baseman's glove.

Freddy said, "Big B from Jamaica originally. Trenchtown, for real."

Leo tried to break the shake, but Bernard held on, maintaining a smile that was fast losing its charm. "What's up, Lee?" he said, and the familiarity unnerved Leo.

"Not much, not much, nice to meet you."

The man threw a shadow on you. He released Leo's hand and Leo took a small step backward to get away from the brutal feel of him. While Leo rubbed his hand, Bernard said to Freddy, "No luck. I'm serious, no spearmint Eclipse. They got Wrigley's Doublemint, Juicy Fruit, they even got Dentyne in there, but no Eclipse. They got Gummi Bears, though."

"Gummi Bears?"

"They chewy."

Freddy said, "Fucking Cuban store don't got no right to call itself convenience." He blew into a palm cupped in front of his face. "Now I'm gonna smell like cheese omelet all morning, shit. Get in, forget it, we already late." He buckled his seat belt, set his coffee in the center console cup holder, and said to Leo, "You got psychiatric problems?"

"What?"

"Don't bullshit me. I know I don't look like no fool to you and don't expect to get treated like one neither, so let's talk straight. What you had in mind when you come 'round here, it ain't no doctor visit. Might be for something else, but we'll leave it like that for the moment. Stick to the job I want done, my advice to you. Everything will go real fucking smooth you just do that." He threw up a hand, thumb and little finger miming a phone. "Expect a call in the next twenty-four to forty-eight." He swiveled his head to the front. "Do it, B. And Lee, enjoy your *pastelitos.*"

The car pulled out and gunned it north, leaving Leo breathing in exhaust fumes, in a black mood.

8

THEY WERE AT CASA GLORIA'S, Oscar's favorite Cuban restaurant. Oscar said, "The man's real name is Osvaldo Herman Massani. His father's an Italian who settled in Cuba in the 1920s, owned a tobacco plantation. Herman came here in late '59, after the fall of Batista. He's been in South Florida ever since, supposedly has family in New Jersey. He's one of those first-generation Cuban-Americans that came in droves and lived amongst each other and didn't feel too compelled to assimilate. His family had money back in Pinar del Río but when Fidel took over he seized their lands, most of their assets, they fled. The Massani family is well connected. Herman's father knew a certain developer's father, this city commissioner's uncle, his mother is cousin to the wife of the ex-mayor of Miami, and the relationships go down the line like that. So Herman is like a lot of Cubans in Miami, only, shall I say, further up the ladder than most."

Patrick said, "So what is he doing in a public hospital like Jefferson?"

"That is what I'm coming to," Oscar said. "Another drink?" He beckoned the waiter.

"I'm good." Patrick put a hand around his martini glass, nearly full, three olives in there the way he liked it. He didn't feel like drinking, had no appetite. The menu was still open in front of him.

"*Bistec de pollo,*" Oscar told the waiter. "*Muchas cebollas*, Ruben. Y *hoy, no quiero arroz blanco, pero congri,* okay?" He raised his empty martini glass. "*Otro mas, por favor.*"

"You were saying about Massani?"

"Massani, Massani," Oscar said. "Eccentric. But well connected. And with all the people he knows he manages to make his political contribution. Which brings us here to you wanting to know who he is, and why he is so important to your campaign."

Patrick cocked his head. "You lost me there. My campaign? I don't even know this man."

Oscar smiled patiently. "But he knows you, my friend." He turned his head to the left. "You see that corridor over there, by the restrooms?"

Patrick nodded, getting impatient with Oscar.

"It leads to a back door. You take that door, walk a few paces and turn left, and you're at the back door to El Rincon, one of the oldest Cuban barbershops in this city. That's the place where Herman Massani used to work."

"That's all well and good and quite charming, but who the hell is he? You still haven't told me."

"He," Oscar said, "is the man we've been searching for these past two weeks. Two nights before you called me, we found him."

"We?" Patrick shook his head. "Who is 'we'? And why are 'we' searching for him?"

"Mr. Massani, my anxious friend, is the man who at this moment is the biggest threat to your campaign."

Patrick tensed up, studied Oscar.

Oscar returned a level gaze.

Patrick reached for his martini and took a deep swallow. Set the glass down and wiped his lips with the cloth napkin, moving slowly and deliberately to conceal his impatience. He ranged the room, a group of men in ties two tables away, two dark-haired young ladies chattering at a center table, silverware clinking all around. A burst of laughter from a far-off table.

Oscar said, "We won't talk about it here. After we eat, we'll go for a walk."

"You'll explain to me about Massani."

"Everything, everything. But get something to eat, please. The food here is too exceptional to pass up and I'm paying, so eat."

Patrick waved the invitation away. "I'm not hungry. I'll need another drink now, though, that's for sure."

One martini later, Oscar had polished his plate and they went for a walk along the concourse of the strip mall. Oscar lit a Montecristo, admiring the smoke rings he sent up into the air. "This is some heat for February, eh?"

"Unseasonable." Patrick walked, hands in pocket.

"What will the hurricane season bring, I wonder? News this morning said fourteen named storms this season. Four will be major hurricanes, but you know how that goes, those forecasts, always inaccurate. I remember in '92, right before Andrew, I told my wife, 'This heat, it must mean something's cooking.' Then, boom, next day the birds begin to fly off, my cat starts to behave strangely, and the next thing, I'm driving to the office and on the radio they're saying the hurricane will hit, the hurricane will hit, landfall expected in two days."

Patrick said, "I'm beginning to feel a different kind of heat at the moment. Oscar, about Freddy Robinson . . . Massani?"

"We are tracking that storm named Massani, don't you worry. As of today, he is merely hovering offshore. Let me tell you, though, your secretary that left, what's-her-name Morales?"

"Gloria Morales."

"Mrs. Morales is under investigation by the election commission. This we know for sure."

"So it's official now. Still, we shouldn't have anything to fear. She has no reason to talk. If she talks, she doesn't get her next severance check, she knows that."

"They're turning the screws on her. They must know she was only a small part. She's naming names. Already they're threatening to interview some of your campaign staff." Oscar motioned for them to veer left, into a breezeway. "We'll go around to the back. I want to show you the barbershop."

Patrick stopped, looked at Oscar nonchalantly puffing his cigar. "How come it's only now I'm hearing about all this? About Massani and the extent of this fucking Morales investigation?"

Oscar turned, lowering the cigar. All traces of good humor gone. "Listen to me. Will you listen to me?"

"I'm listening, Oscar, but you're truly not telling me squat."

Patrick started walking again. Oscar touched him on the shoulder. "Do not worry. We are on the case."

"You've been keeping me in the dark. I don't appreciate that. When did you find out the probe went south?"

"A few days ago. But I'm on the case, *mi amigo*, believe me."

"I need to know absolutely everything about my campaign so I don't feel blindsided, which is what's happening now. If you knew about this Morales thing days ago, why didn't you tell me?"

"Would have served no purpose to worry you, especially since, and I keep saying this, Patrick, I'm working to resolve this thing."

"Yeah? But you still haven't told me just who the hell Massani is."

They passed a nail salon, a shoe store, a liquor store, came out the other end of the breezeway, and turned left, storefronts on one side, parking lot on the other.

"All right, here it is," Oscar said, and they stopped, faced each other. "Gloria Morales was the campaign office contact and Herman Massani was our man in the field. He works in the barbershop and people come to him when they need something done. Like I said, Massani knows everybody, county and city commissioners, school board members, the mayor, you name it. He helps clients sometimes as a favor, most times for a fee. The man knows people, and because he knows all types of people, we hired him. We need votes, he finds voters. If they're not in the city, say for instance they live in Hialeah? He finds a city residence, like Little Havana, the heart of your old district. On paper, that is. All this, only on paper. You know that game, Patrick. If we want voters, he finds a legitimate city address, moves names of people he knows to that city address, and *bam*, we've acquired some votes through absentee ballots, which as you know are harder to track. Not much about this is unfamiliar to you. What I'm sharing with you today is the identity of the man behind it: Herman Massani. Our fixer."

"And you're worried Gloria Morales fingered him and he's going to talk. Not to mention, Freddy Robinson is looking for him. And we have no idea who that scumbag is working for. That's just awesome, Oscar."

Oscar raised a hand. "Patience, *mi amigo.*" They continued past the back door of the Cuban restaurant, two Dumpsters some yards away, a whiff of garbage. Oscar puffed on his Montecristo. "Let's go this way, to the front." They stepped up onto the sidewalk, passed a women's boutique, a UPS Store, and a jewelry shop, Patrick thinking through the mess he was in. He felt it, afraid of this moment, finally asking the big question: "So I take it Massani has actually started to talk?"

"Seems that way. And when we found out and tried to get hold of him, he disappeared. We reached out to his doctor, a certain Alfredo Garrido, but the doctor had conveniently vanished. But not before admitting Massani into a hospital. *That's* why he's at Jefferson."

"Jesus, I don't have to tell you how far this can go, the damage this can cause. This is awful, this, this is a bombshell." Patrick tilted his head back and looked up at the sky. "And of all the fucking places he gets admitted into it's the one where my brother works; I mean, that's just ridiculous."

"Well, you see, that is how Garrido messed up. Massani was in Pine Glade first, up in Boca Raton, and our understanding is something spooked them, probably they learned we had tracked Massani, because we did, and so Garrido moved him. A hospital-to-hospital transfer. Probably they thought that the last place anyone would check is a facility for indigents."

Patrick kept thinking that something else was bothering him, but he couldn't identify it. "Do you know how much Massani has talked?"

"We don't know for sure. Our source on the election commission would only say that Massani has acknowledged there may be some voter fraud and he may know a thing or two about it. Sounds like he's laying the groundwork for a plea deal."

"And who else would want to get ahold of him? I mean to say, who is Freddy Robinson working for, did you find that out? Talk to me, Oscar. Bobby Parra is in prison, but what about Carlos and the other brothers, other family members? Do they know anything about Massani?"

"Slow down and listen to what you're saying, Patrick. Carlos Parra? Carlos is one of *us*, one of the dedicated group of men that's working to put you in the mayor's office. He is the only Parra who knows we're looking for Massani, and he's one of your biggest supporters."

"Okay, so Freddy Robinson working for him wouldn't make any sense, but . . ."

"Carlos says Freddy Robinson used to work for his father and his brother, Bobby, but Carlos says he hasn't had any contact with Freddy Robinson. Doesn't even know where to find him. Unless Carlos is lying, but him being involved? It would be like he was trying to sabotage himself. Still, there are a couple other brothers and a few other cousins and nephews and business partners. So what I'm saying is, Freddy Robinson could be working for any of these people associated with the Parra family."

"So Carlos Parra, the common denominator, doesn't know who Freddy Robinson is working for."

"That's what he says, and he also says he's very worried about his investment in you."

"So it's one of my opponents in the race? One of my political enemies? Whoever it is, Oscar, it's these connections—the Parra family, Freddy Robinson, this man Massani—that I'm very uncomfortable about."

"Speaking of connections: What is that something about your past that Robinson purports to know? Are we ever going to talk about that?"

Patrick ignored him. "This is straight coercion what they're doing here."

"And who do you think *they* are?"

"Hell, since I've been on the commission the list of people I've pissed off is lengthy, and growing."

"Yes, yes," Oscar said, examining the long ash at the end of his cigar. Tapping it off and staring into the distance. "The list may be endless but it's getting late in the game and we can't wait for whoever *they* are to show their faces. You understand? We have to act swiftly, eradicate this cancer. I want you to grasp that."

"Of course, Oscar." Patrick felt tension pushing down on the back of his head. Then he placed it, the other reason for the anxiety that was eating away at him. "Freddy will return with his threats soon. I told my brother to play for time, but we can't wait forever. Tell me what you plan to do about this Massani situation, Oscar."

Oscar drew the cigar from his mouth. "Call your brother as soon as possible, Patrick. Tell him he must keep on waiting, he has to stall, no matter what this Freddy Robinson says. We have a plan in place already, a man who will help us, but we need to keep Massani at that hospital—until we're ready."

Patrick rubbed his eyes with the heels of his palms. "Christ, I need another martini." He exhaled hard and pulled his cell phone from a pants pocket. "I hope my brother's awake. He works nights, sleeps all day."

Oscar said, "I tell you what. I need to make an appointment for a straight-razor shave tomorrow morning. Why don't you meet me inside after you've finished, we'll put our heads together, find out who else might want a piece of Massani? And then afterwards, I'll tell you about this person at the hospital who'll help us. But keep calling your brother until you get through to him." He clapped Patrick on the shoulder and walked off.

Patrick punched in the numbers and lifted the phone to his ear. Waiting for the connection, he said, "Hey, Oscar, I'm wondering about something else."

Oscar turned around and lowered his cigar.

"Investigators must know Massani doesn't really have mental issues, right?"

Oscar smiled. "Everybody knows that. Except the hospital."

Patrick listened to the ring tone, watching Oscar walk away trailing blue-gray smoke. Patrick paced. C'mon, Leo, answer the fucking phone. Turning around, he caught his reflection in the storefront glass and saw his father. It was the phone at the ear, the erect posture, the shadows under the eyes. The resemblance fascinated him. Saddened him, too.

Memories were long and difficult and always lying in wait.

9

EARLY THAT SUMMER after his spring break discovery, the summer the Reverend died, Patrick followed his father two more times. Once to the mystery house on the dark road, and then to a thatch-roof bar on the Western Highway, where the Rev and two Latin teens sat waiting.

Patrick saw the whole meeting from Fonso's pickup in the parking lot, a ball cap tugged low over his eyes. It was obvious from how close they sat that the Rev was meant to be with one of the boys and his father with the other. They drank beers, laughed, the two boys handsome, with big white teeth, broad faces and lanky black hair. They could have passed for twins. An hour drifted by, two. They drank more beers and shots of something. It was all very cheerful and it turned Patrick's stomach. Soon they were the only ones in the bar, a string of multicolored lights along the eaves swaying in the breeze.

Around one A.M., they stumbled out and piled into the Rev's Jag. His father, normally a reserved man, throwing discretion out the window. They took the highway east toward the city and Patrick followed, inky darkness on both sides of the desolate two-lane. Wind blowing into the open windows kept him wide awake.

Patrick had asked Fonso once, a year before, if what they said about the Rev was true, the reason why he left the priesthood and all that. Fonso said he didn't know about no reason he left the Jesuits but he knew what he heard from other cops and what he'd seen himself over the years. "But it's not like the Rev is even trying to hide that shit," Fonso said. "The man don't flaunt it, but he don't go outta his way to cover it up, either."

Patrick asked him like what did he see, and Fonso said, "You really want to know? Naw, man, you don't want to know." Patrick said, Yeah, tell it, modulating the eagerness in his voice. And then Fonso said it. "The Rev likes young boys." Patrick didn't say anything then, but Fonso knew he didn't believe it, and one night he came by Patrick's house in a Belize City Police Land Rover, Fonso in uniform but on dinner break, telling Patrick to hop in quick, he was going to show him something. They drove over the swing bridge to Southern Foreshore, past the courthouse, cut the lights and parked by the seawall. They got out and Fonso led him down a gravel lane between two warehouses and showed him the Rev's Jag, parked in the darkness between two lampposts. "Just watch," Fonso said and they saw two heads in there, one of them smaller. A boy's. A few minutes later they saw the boy's head go down and the Rev holding him there. It was obvious even in the dark. Patrick worrying they were too close to the car, while inside the Rev threw his head back with pleasure. You could hear the groans through the open window and the Rev encouraging the boy. *Juega con el, sí, sí!*

Patrick was following that Jag now, head filled with dark imaginings of his father and the pretty Latin boys. His heart was an anchor, and more than anything, more than the sadness he felt for his mother, he was ashamed.

In Belize City, the Jag stopped at the Byron Hotel on Regent

Street West and he parked close to the open drain and watched them enter the lobby one by one. He felt like he was in a dream, two o'clock in the morning, alone outside a sleazy hotel on a backstreet observing this betrayal, this crime. These boys were even younger than Leo.

He knew he could never tell Leo. He couldn't tell his mother, either, even if part of him suspected she might know already. What good would come of that? So who could he tell?

For days he felt like he was going to explode. Leo would talk to him about his graduation parties, how the prom committee was holding prom after graduation so the school couldn't ban them from serving alcohol, saying, "You could swing by if you want," and Patrick said, "What . . . I'm sorry. What you say?" Totally distracted.

He could hardly stand to look at his father. Told the man he was sick and stayed home from helping him at the dealership. It dawned on him that somebody else probably already knew. Somebody like Fonso. Cops see it all, but the city was so rife with bribes and kickbacks and cops looking the other way that many influential people committed crimes both petty and serious and never smelled the dank of a cell. His father, too, had greased some palms in his day.

In the end, Patrick vowed never to tell anyone what he'd seen.

UNTIL EARLY one Sunday morning, when he woke up before dawn. Padding down the stairs, running shoes in hand, he thought he heard a sound from the living room, poked his head in, saw nothing, and went into the kitchen. He came back out with a glass of orange juice, and now he was sure he heard something.

He followed the sound of ice tinkling in a glass, into the living room, and there, cloaked in darkness, his father sat in his club chair holding a drink. A bottle of Johnnie Walker Black stood by his feet.

Patrick inched closer. "Dad?"

His father sipped his drink. He looked up, eyelids heavy.

"Dad?"

His father turned his gaze to the floor.

It spilled out of Patrick. He'd been holding it in since spring break and now he couldn't stop himself. "Dad, I know, all right?" His father was a statue. Patrick set his glass down on a side table, dropped his shoes, and stood in front of the man. "I know about you, about you and those Salvadoran boys or Honduran or whatever the hell they are, I know," and his voice cracked and he started to cry, swiping hard at the embarrassing tears.

He told his father everything he'd seen, and when his father tried to talk Patrick told him to shut up, let him finish, goddammit let him finish. . . . His father begged him to keep his voice down, but he listened, didn't deny anything. He kept taking quick sips of his drink, unable to hold eye contact.

He said, "Patrick, I'm sorry you saw. . . . Son, I'm in a pickle . . ."

"A *pickle?*" Patrick almost laughed.

". . . and this is not about my reputation or hurting you boys and your mother, hell, if that's not bad enough." Patrick's father swallowed hard and reached for his drink but it was empty. "I have a dilemma. Okay? That's why I'm out here trying to figure out what I should do when I should be in my bed sleeping. The stress this man has put on me."

"What man?"

His father poured whiskey into his glass and stood up. "Forgive me, son. I don't know what else to say." He walked past him into the kitchen.

"What man?"

His father kept going. He returned with ice in the glass and sat down again. That's when he told Patrick about the Reverend, the man he'd trusted for years, to his own detriment, he said. "He got arrested a couple days ago. You wouldn't have heard. No one ever hears about it when he gets in a bind. But your friend paid me a visit yesterday and gave me some news."

"What friend?"

"The policeman. Alfonso."

"Fonso never said anything to me."

"Why would he? What he had to say doesn't concern you."

Patrick stared at his father. "I'm twenty years old, I'm your eldest. I'm part of this family and I've worked enough days with you to know your car business. Do I look naïve to you?"

His father sucked down his drink and splashed more whiskey in the glass. He swirled the drink, studying it. "For chrissake, sit down, Patrick."

Patrick pulled up a dining chair.

His father watched him, screwing the cap on the bottle, searching Patrick's eyes. "You can guess why the Rev was arrested. I don't need to go into details. Well, it's like this. . . ." He wiped his lips, tried again. "It's like this. Whenever he's been in trouble before, the Rev, he and the police superintendent have an arrangement that the Rev pays him a fee for the arrest to disappear." He stopped abruptly. Exhaled, looked down at his feet.

"Fees vary according to what the charges may be, or how greedy the superintendent is at the time. It's been going on like this for years and I've known about it for years, but this time when he got arrested . . ." Patrick's father looked up, shaking his head. "This time the superintendent won't play the game anymore. He has bigger fish to fry."

"What do you mean, bigger fish?"

"Me."

"He wants to come after *you*? Why?"

Ivan Varela dropped his forearms on his thighs, hung his head. A tired man.

Patrick said, "It's because of the cars? They can't get you for anything there so they're coming after you another way?"

His father lifted his drink off the floor and examined it. "According to what Alfonso is saying. They're not picky anymore. They're putting pressure on the Rev." Patrick's father finished his drink and said, "That son of a bitch, he plans to set me up," and rose and went to look out the French doors.

Patrick watched him standing there. Reddish daylight breaking on the water. Pelicans on the posts of a distant pier. Patrick got up, stood next to him. "They want to set you up with . . . young guys? Then that means they can't, because you're not gonna do that anymore." He looked at his father. "Right, Dad? Please tell me yes." His voice quavering again.

"Helping the Rev pay off the superintendent for years, *years*, and for what? Because he's my friend? I've depended on this man like no other, and that son of a bitch, that slick son of a bitch . . ."

Patrick hated seeing his father like this, and for the first time he felt himself hating the Reverend. "So what—what are you going to do?"

His father, gazing out over the yard, said, "I'm just grateful I can talk to you, son."

Patrick hesitated, put a hand on his father's shoulder. "Dad? I'll help you—and anytime you want to talk, okay?"

He heard a door opening behind them. His mother came out of her bedroom closing the front of her housecoat. Patrick had turned around, but his father kept staring outside.

She sat in a chair across the living room, legs slanted to the side, slippers dangling off her toes. She was clutching a wad of tissue. "Have you decided what you're going to do, Ivan?"

Ivan Varela, staring outside, shook his head.

Patrick's mother put her chin in her hand and lowered her eyes. "I've been thinking, and I've come to the conclusion that you've got to face the hard truth. No more lying to yourself."

Patrick looked at his mother, his father. Confused.

She said, "Put that lamp on, will you, Patrick?"

Patrick snapped on a side table lamp. In the light he could see she'd been crying.

Patrick's father left the door, sat slowly in his chair.

She said to him, "Pour me a drink."

He looked at her curiously for a second, but he started pouring the scotch into his glass.

"That's good right there." She reached out. He had to get up to hand her the drink.

"Patrick," she said, "have a seat." She took a neat sip. Drew her legs up under her and regarded the two of them. "I've been thinking about this, Ivan, and the solution to this problem lies in our resolve. Now, if you need resolve, you have only to take a moment and look at all you have here, all that you've worked hard for, this grand old house we bought, that gorgeous view out there. We have a son in college, about to earn a degree, and another one getting ready to head off to college. We have money in the bank, an Australian vacation planned, mutual funds, real estate investments. We're living comfortable and happy lives, aren't we?"

"Yes . . ." Ivan Varela cleared his throat. "Yes, we are."

"Along comes somebody who threatens to topple our cart, drag our names through the mud. Who wants to help put you in jail. What are we supposed to do? Stand back and watch it happen? I won't. I sacrificed too much in the beginning after we were married, watched and said nothing while you made your deals and stayed out late at night and did god only knows what, and me left to raise our sons all by myself. But it worked out." She sipped the scotch. "And, you know something? It needs to continue working out. I will not go back to scrounging like we did in our early days. I will not lose my house. You have a problem. You need to get rid of the problem. It's not that difficult."

Ivan Varela sat up straight, clearing his throat. "What are you saying, Liza? Talk straight."

She let loose a bark of laughter that alarmed Patrick. She said, "The man who has led a clandestine life for all of his marriage now wants clarity. How ironic, Ivan."

"Liza, listen—"

"No," raising a palm. "*You* listen. You yourself have said he's been cheating you for years but at least you know how much he's skimming, you said. Now he's devising your downfall, and you intend to do nothing? He's a problem that needs to be eliminated once and for all."

She turned to Patrick. "You look uncomfortable. Don't be. You're old enough now, as you always like reminding me. You've enjoyed the benefits of being in this family, now it's time to accept the burdens."

She said to her husband, "It would be best if as few people as possible know about this. We need to act fast, and I have no worry that you will. Resolve, Ivan. That's what's required."

She tossed back the drink, banged the glass on the table, and dropped her feet to the floor. "Now, if you'll excuse me, it's Sunday, and Sunday is my tennis day. If you make omelets, Ivan, don't forget I like green peppers in mine. And Swiss, I don't like that provolone you use."

Ivan Varela sat frowning at the empty glass of scotch his wife had just downed at six in the morning. With his two-day beard, he looked shipwrecked.

Patrick's eyes followed his mother until she disappeared into her room. He sat there, stunned. Neither of them spoke. A clock ticked loudly in the kitchen. He was trying to come to terms with what he'd just heard.

It would take him several years.

10

LEO SAW THE MESSAGE LIGHT BLINKING when he got out of the shower, a towel around his waist. He hit the button. The robotic voice droned: Message, received, at, two, thirty, nine, P.M. "Leo, it's me, Patrick. Call me back. This is urgent."

Leo muttered, "What now?" and dialed Patrick's number. He took the phone into the bathroom and came out combing his hair saying, "Well, they haven't called me yet. But if they call and tell me it's tonight, what then?"

"Stall," Patrick said, "stall."

"For how long?"

"Until I tell you otherwise."

"I hope you know what you're doing."

There was a silence. "Don't you worry about me, Leo."

Leo wanted to say, It's not you I'm worried about.

He drove to work that night tempted to light up a joint, bliss away all the Massani worries. Instead he followed the path of reason. Maybe on his break he'd indulge.

The swirl of work distracted him: two admissions, paperwork to prepare for one patient's CT scan, another's ECT. Then he had to order two patients out of the TV room, lock the door, and direct them to bed. One of the patients was Reynaldo Rivera, the spitter. He was freshly shaved and cleaned up now, smiling at Leo as he walked to his room. Leo also locked the linen closet because the other new patient had already shown an affinity for curling up on the shelf under fresh sheets.

Leo did rounds at 11:45, closing doors, flicking off lights. Massani had been released from seclusion and was asleep in 308, a private room. Under Dr. Burton's orders, the evening-shift nurses had dosed the old man with heavy sedatives. So it was twenty patients and all quiet on the psych ward.

Leo hung the clipboard in the nurses' station and tried to ignore how close to each other Martin and Rose were sitting, conversing as softly as lovers. Maybe they had hooked up already? Could be . . . but who cares? Leo had too much on his mind to bother about them.

The phone rang and Rose answered, then turned to Leo. "For you."

He took the phone. "Hello?"

"Listen up, 'cause this'll be quick," Freddy said. "You listening?"

"Yeah, go ahead."

"We'll do this thing tonight."

"Tonight?" Leo glanced sideways at Rose and Martin, walked out of the nurses' station, stretching the phone cord as far as it would go around the corner. "You need to give me better warning, man. How am I supposed to—"

"You're not fucking listening. You're talking shit. Finding excuses, I ain't even trying to hear that. What time's the other tech on break?"

Leo took a deep breath. "He's got first break. So that's midnight."

"Naw, that's not good. How about the head nurse?"

"Last break, four o'clock."

"Perfect. Then that's the time. Here's what's gonna happen. When she goes on break, you place a call to this number, write it down."

"Hold on." Leo went back inside for a pen and sheet of paper, playing along. "Go ahead." He scribbled fast, went back outside. "Then what?"

"You call me so I know it's all cool. Five minutes later, I'll call your nurses' station there. What's the name of the other tech? Martin?"

"Yes."

"Good. If he don't answer, I'll ask to speak to him. I'll be a family member of a patient there or something. Give me the name of a black patient, quick."

"Dolores Washburn."

"All right, Dolores Washburn. So now, while I'm talking to Martin, here's what you do. You go get Mr. Massani and escort him off the floor and down the back stairwell. Don't worry, I know where it is, and I know you don't need to walk by no nurses' station to get to it. You take him to where it leads out to the doors by that lobby with the pharmacy there. You walk him straight out that door. A car'll be waiting at the curb. You leave him, turn around, get your ass back upstairs. The rest will be taken care of, no more concern of yours. You understand everything?"

"Yeah, but—"

"No fucking but. Don't screw this up, now. Lemme repeat this quick so me and you on the same page, chapter, verse and shit." Freddy started at Leo's four o'clock call and reeled off the plan again. Then he said, "Clear?"

Leo felt a stab of anger in his chest, pressure building in his throat, but forced himself to stay calm. "Clear."

"Your night to shine, brother," and Freddy hung up.

Leo walked directly into the conference room, closed the door, and dialed Patrick's cell phone.

Patrick answered after two beeps.

Leo said, "Yeah, it's me. We have a little problem, exactly what I feared might happen. They want him out tonight."

"Tonight? Wait one second." Some shuffling, background noise, a door opening and closing: Patrick leaving the bedroom. "Tonight, you say?"

Leo told him about the call, all the details. "There's more. Freddy knows Massani is out of seclusion, he knows the layout of the floor, even knows the name of the other tech on night shift. The guy's been doing his homework. So I think this is serious now and I just need to know if your plan remains the same. Just calling to make completely sure."

A silence. Patrick mulling it over. "I'll call you back, all right? Give me five minutes."

Leo rang off, poked his head out the door to see if anyone missed him. He had no idea what Patrick was planning, but after tonight, Leo would not be taking orders from him anymore, or from felonious Freddy Robinson. Maybe that meant Massani would need to go somewhere else, leave the hospital on his own terms. Maybe Leo was just the man to arrange that, and give Patrick and Freddy the finger.

After an eternity, the phone rang again. He answered, "Annex Three, may I help you?"

"Here's what I want you to do," Patrick going straight to the point. "Tell Freddy when you call him at four that Massani is giving you trouble, he's acting up and there's too much heat so you'll have to try again tomorrow night. That man absolutely cannot leave that floor tonight. Under no circumstances."

"So tell Freddy tomorrow instead, you sure about this?"

"Final word, I'm sure."

So that was that.

LEO DID all the half-hour rounds from then until 3:30, which gave him the opportunity to pace. Now and then, he'd hit the bathroom for a nerves-induced leak. Now and then, a patient would shuffle out of a room to a water fountain, slurp, shuffle back in. Otherwise, the floor was dark and quiet, Martin writing notes, Rose watching him. Leo wondered how he'd tell Freddy, if he'd sound cool or if he'd hesitate. He wanted to sound natural.

At 4:10, Rose took her break, toting blanket and pillow to the conference room.

At 4:16, satisfied she wasn't coming out anytime soon, Leo dialed Freddy's number, stretched the cord out the door and around the corner. "Yo, man, it's me." He paused, trying to relax. "Look, we can't do this thing tonight. Massani's been acting up something awful, really paranoid, you know? And they're keeping a close eye on him." A glance over the shoulder at Martin. "In fact, the other tech here, Martin? He's basically babysitting Massani, making sure his behavior doesn't escalate. So tonight's not gonna work. Let's try again tomorrow, same time."

Freddy said, *"Reeeally."* It wasn't a question. He said it like a man talking to a child. "Really, now."

"Yeah."

"Tomorrow, uh? Wouldn't that be cool. Now listen to me, 'cause I'm going to say this only once: Don't lie to me. You don't think I know your voice by now? I know when you're spouting a falsehood, Lee. This ain't no fucking game, Lee. This man's stepping off that floor *tonight.* You never heard me ask your opinion in the matter, so you coming with this suggestion right here is bullshit I got no interest in. You got fifteen fucking minutes to get the man off that floor, feel me?"

The line went dead, and Leo resisted the urge, barely, to slam that phone down. He slipped into the bathroom, took yet another leak, washed his hands and splashed water on his face. He paper-toweled dry, looking at himself in the mirror. Flecks of gray hair on the sides. Crow's-feet. He did feel old tonight. Man, he despised Freddy.

He paced the hallway with the rounds board again. A bear in a cage.

At 4:28, the nurses' station phone rang. He walked by the door and continued down to the men's side. The phone kept ringing, then he heard Martin's voice. "Annex Three, this is Martin, may I help you?" Leo walking on, reaching the door at the end of the hall, turning around in the darkness, hearing, "Mrs. Washburn? May I ask who's speaking, please? No, sir, your aunt hasn't been discharged. . . ." Leo watching the rectangle of light from the nurses' station, hearing Martin say, "I'm not sure why anyone would say that. . . . That's right. It's Dr. Burton." Leo keeping still, listening to Martin going, "Yes. . . . Uh-huh. . . . Yes. . . . No, sir," Freddy yakking it up, keeping him on the phone, thinking Leo was doing the deed.

A long five minutes later, Leo heard Martin hang up and saw him come to the doorway and look both ways, Leo quickly pretending to check the bathroom, feeling he could breathe again.

Fuck you, Freddy. That's all I got to say.

LEO STARTED feeling calmer just before dawn. He'd been so keyed up he hadn't taken a break. First time in years. He was still pacing the hall when he heard someone talking in one of the male rooms. He tracked the voice to a room on the right, slowing down to determine which one. He opened the doors, peering in, happy to find something else to occupy his mind.

A room door on the right opened and a patient trekked out, tugging at his droopy hospital-issue pajama pants, flip-flops slapping down the hall toward the bathroom. He swung open the bathroom door, the light inside illuminating the face of the new patient, Reynaldo Rivera.

Leo followed to check that all was fine, heard the man talking to himself in one of the stalls, probably hallucinating. Leo saw the stall door open, Reynaldo's back turned to him, the man whistling a tune now.

Around six, Leo traipsed into the nurses' station and started morning preparations. He broke out a new sheet of patients' names for morning vital signs, wheeled two blood-pressure machines out into the hallway, a table, and two digital thermometers. Martin helped Rose set up the medication cart and rolled it just outside the door.

Pretty soon patients were wandering the hallway. At six-thirty,

Leo picked up the microphone and switched on the intercom. "Goooood morning, patients," his voice booming over ceiling speakers all down the hall, "it's time to rise and shine and come and get your vital signs taken. Today is February sixteenth, Thursday, and that means it's linen change day, so after vital signs, strip your beds of all linen and that means you, too, Frances Hoy. Come to the nurses' station for vital signs, everyone."

Here's where things got hairy, change of shift, night staff getting ready to leave and day staff strolling in. A time for patients to take advantage of the confusion—to elope, maybe sneak into each other's beds or try something in a bathroom stall.

Now patients were trickling out of their rooms, some yawning, hair messy, eyes sticky. Some formed a line, others stood around scratching themselves. A couple of day-shift nurses pushed through, saying excuse me, morning, slipping into the locker room off the hall to punch time cards, then going to the staff room to pour coffee, finish their makeup.

Rose took blood pressures, Leo handled temps, Martin recorded the readings.

After a while, Rose said, "So who's left to do?"

"Lemme see." Martin going down the list with a finger. "Cenovia Delgado. . . . Frances Hoy, so what else is new? . . . Herman Massani, and who else? . . . Reynaldo Rivera . . . that's it."

"Can I have some cranberry juice?" A female patient getting into Leo's air space.

Leo took a backward step into the nurses' station. "In a little bit, Dolores," reaching for the microphone and snapping on the intercom. "Cenovia, Frances, Herman, and Reynaldo, please report to the nurses' station, we need to get your vital signs."

Dolores said, "That boy Reynaldo loves him some Herman. All morning I see him he looking at the old man."

"Really? Do me a favor, Dolores, don't block the doorway, please. I'll get everybody some juice soon as I'm through here."

"The man got a cell phone, too. I seen it."

Leo, arranging charts alphabetically, looked up. "Which man has a cell phone?"

"You gonna get me my juice?"

"Of course, but tell me, Dolores, who has a cell phone, now?"

"Reynaldo. He got a visitor yesterday gave it to him. Think I didn't see? They slip it to him under the table in the dining room, a woman. I seen them, they think they slick."

Leo moved past her and out into the hallway and looked down to the men's side. He didn't like what he was feeling. He started toward the men's bathroom, saying without looking back, "The only men left for vitals are Herman and Reynaldo, correct?"

Martin said, "That's right."

Leo sure didn't like what he was feeling and hurried past bundles of bedsheets outside the doors. Reynaldo's room door was open, bed not stripped, no one in there. Leo barged into the men's bathroom, one patient taking a shower. He headed for Herman Massani's room now. The door was closed. It wouldn't open, something blocking it from the inside. He put his shoulder into it and pushed, leaned with both palms and pushed harder.

Something scraped the floor, the dresser it sounded like, the door opening a fraction. He walked to the opposite wall, ran to the door and stomped it, the door bucking open, leaving a space wide enough for him to squeeze through. He poked his head in, jammed a shoulder through, saw what was happening and stepped back out and hollered down the hall, "Red code! Red code! Help, red code!" Banging the door against the dresser that was blocking it, shoving his way inside.

Reynaldo was pressing a pillow over Herman's face, the old man clawing at Reynaldo, skinny legs flailing.

Leo shouted, "Stop!" running to grab Reynaldo. Reynaldo stuck out a hand and jabbed Leo in the throat. Leo gagged, backing up. Reynaldo released the old man and pivoted to face Leo.

Right there, something in Reynaldo's eyes turned all icy, and gave him away: Dude was no mental patient. He smiled and punched Leo in the side of the head. Before Leo could raise an arm, Reynaldo hit him solidly in the face, dropped a step back, and Leo charged, reaching for the arms, to immobilize those lightning fists, seeing too late Reynaldo's foot lifting in a roundhouse kick, the leg flying at Leo as he moved his head to the right to evade it, but the foot smacked him in the left temple and fireflies flickered and his vision dimmed, going darker, tunnel vision, and he swooned, felt himself floating . . . no way to stop floating . . .

11

THE DOCTOR'S FACE LOOMED OVER HIM. "Just a tiny pinch, that's all you'll feel." He tipped Leo's head back on the table with a finger and aimed the needle at his chin. Three injections later, chin numb, he lay staring at a lit lamp in the cold room.

The doctor, an East Indian, his breath steely with garlic, leaned over with what looked like a sewing needle now, using a pair of scissors to string the sutures. His name was Dr. Bhatt. Leo didn't know exactly how he knew that. His head was foggy.

Dr. Bhatt positioned the light close. "Okay, here we go. You shouldn't feel a thing."

"How many?" Leo asked.

"About four, maybe five, we'll see."

Dr. Bhatt began stitching him up. Pieces of stray memory floated by and Leo reached for them through a haze.

HE SAW himself in a chair in the psych ward dining room. Bloodstains on his pants, his shoes. His chin throbbing.

People milling about in front of him. Techs, nurses. Jesus, his head ached.

A doctor arrived and huddled to one side with the nurses. Leo's left ear was ringing, he couldn't hear a thing. He opened and closed his jaw a few times. The techs started leaving, no more work for them here, Reynaldo in seclusion already.

Someone put a hand on his shoulder. Martin. "How you feeling?"

"Not too smart."

"Transportation will arrive in a sec. Hang in there."

"Transportation?" Leo had to lean back to look at him.

Martin seemed amused. "To get you stitched up, Leo, have the doctor look at you. You were out about three minutes, man. Completely out. You had us worried."

They wheeled him out on a gurney and he remembered going down in the elevator, looking up at the face of the young black orderly with a pencil-line mustache.

When he opened his eyes again he was talking to the doctor he knew as Bhatt, who was telling him he'd split his chin when he fell on the floor and in the future he really should be more careful whom he picked fights with.

Tittering at this attempt at humor.

LEO LEFT Dr. Bhatt's office with four stitches under his chin and a small bottle of ibuprofen. It was 11:10; he should have been home hours ago. Tessa would be worried. When he got home he'd say . . . what? He'd say, Hey, listen . . .

No matter what he said, the result would be the same: stress for her and the baby. She was already fretting about their finances, their future, and he couldn't disagree, he needed to begin hunting for other opportunities instead of merely talking about it, especially since this job exposed him to kung fu motherfuckers posing as mental patients who found pleasure in kicking him silly.

All of this, plus a certainty now: Reynaldo Rivera had been put on the ward for one thing only, and that was to make sure Herman Massani left the hospital as a dead man. Leo thought, Would you listen to yourself? Your imagination's running away with you, son.

But he knew it wasn't. This was serious and it was freaking him out, and what was worse, he suspected Patrick was involved, telling him to stall, keep Massani on the floor. Why? Because Patrick knew what was going to happen. But the piece that didn't fit: Reynaldo was admitted to the hospital before Leo ever went to Patrick with this Massani problem, so how could Patrick have arranged to fix a problem he wasn't aware of yet? The clearest part of this fuckery was people wanted to kill this old man Massani, and he, Leo Varela, a laid-back dude who just wanted to smoke a little weed now and then and write some poetry, was smack in the middle of the shit. Man, this was so twisted.

All this was running through his head as he cut through the parking lot heading for his car, so he saw them too late. Freddy and Bernard, arms folded, leaning against the black Benz, watching him come. Leo said under his breath, "Like I need any more drama this morning," but he kept moving.

Freddy called, "Good morning, or maybe I should say afternoon. And here I am thinking all these evil thoughts, telling my man Big B here for sure you pussied out and hauled ass through a back exit or somethin'. But no, the hero appears. What you wearing on your chin, dawg?"

"Got assaulted by a patient last night," Leo said, walking up, "on top of all that shit with the old man I told you about. I had to get stitches, too," pointing to his chin and shaking his head. "Really sorry, man, but like I said, tonight we try again, if you want."

The Benz was parked at a tight angle next to his Corolla, blocking his driver's-side door. The sun was out strong, a few stragglers in scrubs hurrying across the parking lot to the annex. For the first time in hours, Leo felt alert. Maybe that was because something in their posture, the way these two were staring, felt like a threat.

He said, "Hey, I tried, but it was just one of those things, unexpected." Pointing to his chin again. "Four stitches."

Freddy nodded, looking off to the side. He plucked the front of his shirt away from his body and flapped it. "Hot like a bitch this morning. Let's talk inside the car. Much more comfortable."

Bernard unlocked the car with his key chain remote and opened a back door. Freddy slipped inside and scooted down to make room for Leo.

Standing there. Thinking, Better not get in that car. Thinking of a way to refuse without looking scared. He fished his keys from a pocket and said, "Man, Fred, I've got to book. Got to take my fiancée for her pregnancy checkup this morning, and I'm running late as it is."

Bernard stood arms folded at the door, chin tilted up, looking down his nose at Leo.

Freddy said, "Get in, Lee, this'll take two minutes. I got errands, too, awright? Get the fuck in the car and let's talk right quick."

Bernard said, "You hear the man."

Leo got in, apprehensive. Bernard slammed the door and squeezed into the driver's seat, the car rocking under his bulk. He started the engine, cranked the air.

Leo dropped his hand on the seat, feeling the cool, smooth leather, taking in the rich smell, the car too classy for these two driving it.

Freddy said, "Listen to me, now. I need you to guarantee, okay—*guarantee* that this man is walking out tonight. No excuses, no bullshit, I'm talking results. You hearing me?"

Freddy acting cockier every time they spoke.

"I do, man, just that this was one of those things outta my control, the way the man was behaving. Then I get hit like this, anybody on staff, it means a ton of paperwork for us to fill out, incident reports, insurance stuff. I had absolutely no time."

"Hear me asking questions?" Freddy shook his head. "I don't need no details, all this woe-is-me nonsense. I could give you some rope so you blab on with your little explanation, next thing you hang yourself with it, but, see, I'm gonna save you. Why? 'Cause I got a job to do and that's to make sure you do yours and that's all I care about. You ain't doing yours, so now I end up looking like a fucking idiot. I can't have that no more, dawg. Tonight? You *gots* to come through. This man getting in this car tonight," Freddy jabbing the seat with a finger, "we driving off with him, and you and me and Bernard and everybody else concerned with this bullshit here gonna live happily ever after, the end. Tell me you understand the situation, Lee."

Leo had just about had it with this guy but kept his irritation in check. "Hey, I understand." His eyes moved to Bernard fiddling with something on the front seat.

Freddy said, "Same time, same plan. No change. Except the end result."

"I got it," Leo said, watching Bernard raise something silver, turning around. It was one of those spring-coil grip exercisers, a heavy-duty one, thick coils, knurled silver handles. Bernard squeezed it a couple of times, the handles clicking when they touched. He handed it to Leo.

"Show me what you got."

Leo took it and examined it, looked at Freddy. Freddy was staring off through the window, like he'd seen this show before. Leo squeezed hard, the knurling rough on his skin, Leo bringing the gap to within a half inch before he had to release.

"Not bad," Bernard said, "you almost had it. Ever do this before?"

"Not since high school." Leo handed it back and flexed his fingers. He was ready to leave but Bernard produced another. "Try this one. That's a Number Two. That first one was a Number One. They got like four levels. When you reach the fourth and mash the handles, they call you a Captain of Crush. Try it."

Leo held the gripper, turning it around in his hand to check out the thicker coil.

Bernard said, "The company makes them sends somebody out, verify the feat, then gives you a certificate. Only a few dozen people in the world can mash a Four, know that? That's a serious challenge there, nigger, even that Number Two. Go ahead."

Reluctant, Leo wiped his hands on his pants, squeezed the gripper. Like squeezing a rock at first, the handles creeping in a couple of inches and refusing to go any farther. Veins in his fore-arm popping out. He let go, exhaling hard, a little perspiration prickling his hairline. "Yeah, that's pretty tough," he said, hand-ing back the gripper. "Good luck in your pursuit, Bernard."

The man grinned. "I almost got the Four, almost. Less than a quarter inch. Did it one time, just one time, but it's all good. Training, that's all. Like I got a sick grip now. Check this," stretching an arm across the back of his seat. "This my normal grip, left hand."

Leo slowly brought his left hand up and clasped Bernard's big mitt. The man applied pressure. Leo said, "Yeah, yeah, I feel it." The man increased the squeeze and Leo said, "Easy there." Ber-nard grinned. "You like that?" He squeezed harder and Leo felt his hand being crushed, knuckles grinding. "Okay," he said through his teeth, "ease up . . . ease up . . . point taken." Pain lifted him off the seat, Leo reaching with his other hand to try and pry loose. That only made Bernard bear down more and say, "Siddown." No grin now.

Freddy turned away from the window. "Lee, the thing I want to impress upon you is the significant nature of what I need you to do or you might not take me serious. The man I represent knows it's business, me and Big B here know it's business, and you need to know it."

One more time, Leo tried to grab Bernard's wrist and wrench his hand away before the man splintered it. "Let me go, man . . . let me go."

Freddy said, "You got one more shot, that's tonight."

Leo writhing now, head down, one knee sinking to the floor. Bernard took hold of him with two hands and bent his little finger back, way back, till Leo had to lean back with it so it wouldn't snap . . . so it wouldn't snap . . . so it wouldn't . . . *Fuck*, it snapped loudly, and pain shot up his arm and he heard himself scream. "Ahh, Jesus . . ." He was sweating, could hardly catch his breath.

"Strike one," Freddy said. "That was strike one."

Now Bernard grasped his ring finger and bent it back, Leo saying, "Wait, wait. . . ."

And Freddy saying, "You play games, you get three strikes and you out. Since you obviously like motherfucking games, you need to understand you can't get three strikes with me, no sir."

With a flick of the wrist, Bernard broke the finger and Leo hollered again, throwing his head back.

"Strike two."

Bernard released him with a smile, and Leo dropped his other knee and leaned his forehead against the back of the front seat, hugging the hand close to his chest, sweating. Tears filled his eyes, his nose running uncontrollably. He pulled his chin into his chest and rocked back and forth, the movement seeming to ease the pain, back and forth. He kept telling himself, Come on, control yourself. Control, control. . . . He felt humiliated; at the same time, though, something was steeling inside of him, deep inside, and he lifted himself off the floor. Flopped back on the seat. The air-conditioning chilled him all over. He started to tremble a little, but with deep breaths, slow and deep, he stilled his body.

Freddy tossed a folded handkerchief in his lap. "Clean yourself up."

Leo looked at the hankie on his leg. He picked it up with his good hand, wiped his face. Okay, motherfuckers. This is how it is, huh?

Freddy stared out the window at the nurses, the hospital staff in green scrubs with clipped-on badges flapping as they walked across the parking lot. Bernard looked straight ahead, working one of the grippers, the coil squeaking. Without moving, Freddy said, "Take him to the emergency room, Big B. Tell the man where it is, Lee."

"'Round the corner." Leo dropped his head back and closed his eyes. "Go north on Twelfth, hang a right on Nineteenth Street, couple blocks down to Ninth Avenue, then another right." He winced. "Take another right onto Eighteenth and it's on the right-hand side."

Bernard put the car in reverse and backed out. "One emergency room coming up."

Leo felt the car moving and for a moment he thought he might puke. He shut his eyes tight against the pain and concentrated on his breathing.

"Know something I been checking out? Some fine young women work at this place, Lee. How you get any work done, man? I'd be like *distracted*."

Bernard gave a chuckle. He paid the parking lot attendant and turned toward the main gate.

"Speaking of which," Freddy said, "I tell you about the other night, Bernard? Yeah, man, at Casa Rita's, that club on Lejeune they dance meringue and salsa, all them Latin dances? This Dominican female, rocking body. I was checking her out all night, asking myself, This the one? You want to go through with this? You know, doubting myself. So like I roll up there, she's sitting there with a drink, just got off the dance floor, and I see the dude she was dancing with wasn't her man or nothin', so I roll up and ask her like, Care to dance? Tell her I'd been admiring her all night and would love just one turn on the floor with her, you know? Give her some sweet talk, see how she responds. Shit, bitch acted all cold. Told me like thanks, but no thanks."

"Don't tell me. You picked her."

"Damn right. I say to myself, All right, baby, you the one for me, then. You mine tonight. So I said, Okay, and asked her could I at least buy her a drink? Rum and pineapple juice, you say? Sure, baby. Got me a beer, got her a rum and pine. Started chattin' again with her. You know those club girls like the attention, sitting there all foxy fine in the strapless dress, all glittery, trying to look bored but you *know* she's out fishing, too, which man wouldn't throw his line, don't you agree?"

Bernard shook his head. "So you did it again?"

"What you think?"

"How?"

"Right there at the bar. She wasn't even paying me no mind. Just drop the magic pill in there and like here you go, baby, *salud*, smooth like that."

Bernard shook his head.

"Not even ten minutes later, bitch all groggy, the love potion hitting her nice, woman still refusing to go with me. Tell her, No, sweetie, you need some fresh air, that's why. This loud music and all that alcohol and cigarette smoke doing a number on you, come on with me. Finally, I'm like, Come here, girl, grabbing her real rough-like 'round the arm, see, manhandling her so she know what's up. Got her in the car, drive over to a parking lot behind that liquor store off Seventh Avenue. Man, after that, quick and easy. Except the panties decided to fight back, so it was snip, snip, with my trusty scissors in that glove box right there." Freddy clapped his hands loudly, giggling. "Oooh, baby. Now, that's what I'm talking 'bout!"

They were on Nineteenth Street, Bernard moving into the right lane, indicator on, Ninth Avenue coming up.

Leo thinking, Who is this guy sitting next to me? Was Freddy always this nasty, or was it prison that thoroughly warped him?

"What's that girl name from your college days again, Lee? The blonde used to live in the dorms, acted all hyper when she drank Coke. Samantha?"

Leo gently set the hand in his lap, every movement causing him pain. "Rebecca. Samantha was the roommate."

"Yeah, yeah, *Rebecca*. I had me some Rebecca one night. Remember that 'cause she was the first one tasted my love potion. Know something, come to think of it? Was in your dorm room, Lee. Shit, that was a thrill. Girl was—"

Bernard interrupted, "On the right-hand side, you said?" Bernard searching for Leo's face in the rearview.

"Uh-huh."

Freddy stared hard at the back of Bernard's head. "Bernard don't like hearing this, you know? Can't even share my adventures with him. Dude's a family man, don't want to hear none a that. Bernard don't even drink, Lee. You still don't drink, Bernard?"

Bernard shook his head. "I drink water."

"Don't drink, don't smoke, don't do drugs. Hey," Freddy said to Leo, "think you could find out where I might hook up a batch

a roofies, you work in a hospital and all this? Bernard had connections but the man cut me off."

Leo edged forward on the seat. "You can pull up right here at
the curb." Without looking at Freddy, he said, "Rohypnol is illegal. They don't make it in the U.S."

"You sure? I hear it's illegal *without* a prescription."

"No. You can't buy it here. So you're asking me if I could get
it at the hospital, the answer's no. Other than that, I wouldn't
know how to hook you up."

Freddy stared at him.

Leo pitched the handkerchief on the seat and reached his
good hand over to open the door.

"You beginning to sound like your brother," Freddy said, "a
real fucking know-it-all."

The car rolled up the curving trauma center sidewalk, people
in green or mauve scrubs hustling by, a couple of black and Hispanic women holding babies sitting on a bench outside the
emergency room. He opened the door and stepped out, Freddy
saying something he couldn't hear, but he refused to turn around.
Freddy shouted his name and said, "Cooperation, that's the key
word . . . ," and something else, but Leo had already blocked
Freddy out and the words disappeared in the voices and footsteps on the sidewalk and car horns and an ambulance racing
up—and his mad heart hammering in his ears.

Going through the automatic doors to the emergency room,
he met the orderly who had wheeled him off the annex that morning. He was pushing an old lady in a wheelchair. "You all right,
player?" he said, looking Leo up and down. "Day-um, what
happened to your hand?"

Leo straightened his shoulders and tried to relax the grimace. "Another rough day at the office. I was pressing down too hard with a pen and broke a couple digits," and he raised his left hand, getting his first good look at the twisted fingers.

He walked into the lobby, holding the hand loosely. It was already crowded in there. Waiting to see the nurse, he started trembling again. Feeling like he could kill somebody.

12

T HE BEST SHAVE IN TOWN, trust me on this," Oscar said as the barber reclined the chair.

Patrick's barber did the same to his and lathered his face with warm shaving soap from a white bowl, swirling it on in circular motions with the badger brush. Then he picked up a gleaming straight razor and whipped it back and forth on a strop hanging off the chair arm. Patrick and Oscar could see each other in the mirror, barbers' capes tucked under necks, the clock on the wall behind them, the front door locked because the shop was temporarily closed to other customers.

Oscar said to his barber, an old Cuban, "I've been waiting all morning for this. This is a day's growth."

"Is perfect. Thick is good, the shave is closer."

The other barber, a younger, dapper guy in a black smock, tipped Patrick's head back gently with a finger under the chin and leaned in with the straight razor. Starting from the sideburns, the barber scraped downward, pausing to wipe the blade on a towel, continuing along the jawline and the chin. Patrick had gone to an expensive shop in Bal Harbour for a shave once, a men's boutique they called it, but this experience was superior, what with the hot towels they'd begun the process with, the shaving oil massaged in to lubricate and warm the skin, and that badger brush and real old-fashioned shaving bowl; you couldn't make it any more satisfying.

He was enjoying the lull before the meeting. Oscar was in heaven over there, eyes closed, a little smile. He said something to the barber in Spanish, then said to Patrick, "Fourteen strokes. A professional shave, fourteen give or take a few." Peering sideways at the barber, "*Verdad*, Lazaro?"

Lazaro nodded. None of the barbers had said much. They had opened the place an hour early, locked it again, fixed a pot of Cuban coffee, and served it in espresso cups. A special service that was expected.

Fourteen strokes. Just like Oscar to know some arcane fact like that. He approached matters mathematically, with a cool head, you had to give the man his due, whipping out a legal pad last night in his office in Coral Gables, drawing lines down a page and saying, "Common factors. You're thinking what I'm thinking, I hope. Let's examine the links."

Patrick saying, "All right, then. We have Freddy Robinson, Herman Massani, and me and . . . Mr. or Mrs. X."

Oscar wrote each name in a separate column. "But this X must be a known quantity. I've spoken to all the Parras, every brother, cousin, sister, nephew, aunt, and such who was in any way associated with old Alejandro's businesses and who, it's reasonable to believe, would know of Freddy Robinson, and I must say, I keep coming back to one name, the only logical connection but which doesn't add up."

"And that's . . . ?"

"Carlos Parra."

"My biggest booster."

"And the only one who knows you and Herman Massani and has any kind of connection to Freddy Robinson. But, yes, it doesn't make sense. He says he knows Freddy Robinson but has had no personal dealings with him. I tried not to push, didn't want to alarm him, didn't want to reveal too much of what's happening, of course, in the event he really has nothing to do with this."

"You believe him?"

Oscar sighed, put the pen down. "I don't know. That's the problem. Carlos isn't like the rest of his family. You know him, low profile, Harvard grad, cerebral guy. But, ah, my instincts tell me to take the simplest, most obvious possibility and try to suss out the answers later, so that would mean . . ." He picked up the pen and scribbled fast.

Patrick read off the page, "Carlos Parra is Mr. X."

Oscar sat back and stared at the names on the page. "What are you thinking, tell me. I can feel you thinking."

"Here's my question: Could it be someone who knows all the names here, knows me? Doesn't like me, perhaps has a major problem with me? A political enemy?"

Oscar's pen hovered over the page. "Who? Who, of all the people who've had major disagreements with you, knows all three of these other names?"

Patrick shifted in his chair and gazed out the window at the lamplit circular driveway. "There's . . . No, he doesn't know Freddy. . . ."

"A business competitor, another lawyer, maybe?"

Patrick nodded. "Possibly. . . ." He sat forward. "Listen, Carlos's company, Seacrest Developments, who are the partners?"

Oscar tapped the pen on the page. "I believe it's only one person, a man named Rocha, Silvero Rocha."

"Rocha? As in the Rocha family that owns those condos on Brickell Avenue?"

"One of the sons, but this one used to develop business parks, I understand."

"Interesting that he doesn't work with his family."

"He can't. They sold the business a few years ago. A company called Pitts and Newberg, he was with Pitts before they went belly-up."

"Pitts folded?" Patrick sat back. "About two years ago Pitts came before the commission wanting to put a business park off U.S. 1, backing up to this residential neighborhood. Had the residents all up in arms. The rezoning request went to a vote on the planning and rezoning board; I was on the board. I basically didn't like the idea from the start, everybody knew that. I made sure my constituents knew that. I argued against the request, changed some minds on the board. We voted to turn the request down. Now you're saying this is the same Pitts and Newberg Rocha worked with?"

Oscar leaned back in his chair and smiled.

Patrick stood and went to the window. "And Rocha is Carlos's business partner," he said to himself. He turned around. "Then he is the one. Silvero Rocha is the one we need to talk to."

Oscar circled Rocha's name and drew an array of lines from Carlos Parra to Silvero Rocha, Freddy Robinson, and Herman Massani. He sat back and admired the web. "Right here in black and white. See how easy that was? Let's give Mr. Rocha a call."

HE ARRIVED at twelve-thirty, like he said he would. A heavy-set bodyguard with a smoothly shaved head followed him into the barbershop. Rocha was a small man with rimless glasses and a neatly trimmed gray beard that lent him an air of distinction. His style was all business, dark brown striped suit over light brown shirt, chocolate tie. A gold Rolex jangled on his wrist when he moved, or more like swaggered. Flashy, bantam rooster—these were the words that came to mind when Patrick shook his hand. Greetings exchanged all around, stiff smiles, the bodyguard standing off to one side.

Lazaro the barber asked would *Señor Rocha quiere un cafecito?* Rocha said no thanks and addressed the big man. "Bernard? Coffee and a shave?"

Bernard passed a hand over his jaw, smiling. "You saying I need one, Mr. Rocha?"

Rocha smiled back and waved it off.

Bernard picked up a magazine and moved to take a seat. "My wife says I'm handsome just like this, better not risk it."

Patrick watched the man's too-loose short-sleeve shirt that would have been tucked if not for the firearm on his right hip it was concealing, Patrick discerning the outline of the gun, a full-sized pistol, maybe a Glock, like all these black guys.

Oscar said, "Let's convene in the back, gentlemen," leading the way past the restroom on the right and down a narrow hallway past a storage room. They entered a windowless room with a long conference table and plush leather chairs. Off to one side behind swing doors was a kitchenette. "Before we begin," Oscar said, "can I get anyone a drink?"

"I'm quite all right," Rocha said. He unbuttoned his suit with a flourish and sat down. At the head of the table.

Patrick sat to his left. Oscar returned from the kitchen with two bottled waters, handed one to Patrick.

"So." Oscar sat across from Patrick.

"So, Oscar." Rocha grinned, teeth bleach-white.

"We have business to discuss."

"We do indeed. I was wondering how long you were going to take to reach out to me."

Oscar twisted the cap off his bottle. "You could've revealed yourself earlier. Just a thought." He drank some water.

"Now, that wouldn't be a smart way to negotiate. A man like you, I don't have to remind you about strategy."

Oscar capped his bottle and said, "All due respect, Silvero, you and me, we might know the same people but we never had the pleasure of doing business. How would you know what kind of man I am?"

Rocha leaned his forearms on the table, making a show of looking at both men. "We are businessmen. Aren't we businessmen? Of course we are. We understand self-interest. Capitalism. Politics," a smile Patrick's way. "We all want a piece of the pie, a fair piece. That's better for everyone. Nothing too big, but an adequate piece nonetheless."

"There are some," Oscar said, rotating his chair slowly, "who might say, considering what has brought us together today, that you haven't played fair, sir, that you're siding in. Obviously, it's through your business partner that you came to know about Herman Massani and his relation to us. Question is, does Carlos know what you're doing? You're putting yourself in a tight spot. You're squeezing into an agreement between friends."

Rocha shook his head. "Friends. That word has caused businessmen more grief than any word in the English language. I didn't come here to discuss friendship. I came to discuss business. We want something from each other. Let's put our ideas to work and hammer out a deal. Like businessmen."

Oscar studied Rocha, eyes traveling from the fine cut of the suit to the neat beard. "If it weren't for the fact you may be right, I'd consider that absolutely lacking in respect. How can you be so certain that we're not the kind of men to see to it you pay dearly for the shit you're trying to pull?"

Rocha said, "If I didn't know the men I was dealing with, I'd consider that a threat, Oscar."

Patrick raised a hand and leaned in. "Please, let's all calm down here."

"But we are calm," Rocha said, all cool, folding his hands in his lap.

"Can we take a couple steps back and consider what we're saying here?"

"And what are we saying, Mr. Varela?" Rocha's level gaze on him.

Patrick stared back at the man. "That we're businessmen. Engaged in a transaction."

Rocha looked at Oscar. "You see, I like the way Mr. Varela's thinking." He pointed at Patrick. "Straight to the point, that's admirable."

Patrick said, "What is it you want?"

Rocha kept nodding. Business frown on, he returned his elbows to the table. "The county will be putting out bids for the airport construction, after the election. I want some of the action there. In the past my projects have met with, let's call it resistance, from certain commissioners. Mainly you. I want you to understand, I intend to throw a lot of support behind you now, monetary and however else you might see fit, help you become mayor."

Oscar said, "Did our mutual friend tell you how important Herman Massani is to us?"

Rocha swiveled his chair and faced Oscar squarely. "Our friend Carlos Parra is the product of a dysfunctional family. The man does dysfunctional things. People seem to think he's different from the rest of them, all those sad brothers and relatives, but no . . . oh, no. Carlos has his own demons."

He reached into a back pocket and pulled out his wallet. He slipped out and unfolded two checks and laid them on the table in front of Oscar. "I keep these on me as a reminder about friends. About trust. These canceled checks, these are Seacrest Developments checks. Can you read the signatures?"

Oscar leaned over, squinted at them. "Looks like Carlos Parra's to me."

"Carlos Parra. That's right. Do you see whom they're made out to?"

"Says . . . Atlantic Storage."

"Atlantic Storage, yes. Problem is, that's a dummy company. An old building in Little Havana. A legal address, that's it. No real business. Twelve thousand dollars to a dummy company. You know who set up this company? Carlos Parra. You know why? Because he was trying to scam me. He has a gambling problem, you see. Huge debts. So he writes up invoices for phony services, pays them off to this company, and pockets the money. And he thought for some bizarre reason that I wouldn't find out."

Rocha picked up the checks and stared at them. "What happened when I confronted him—well, you can imagine." He tapped his temple. "You see how some men think? What drives people to such risks? Is it in their nature?" He shook his head, returned the checks to his wallet and jammed the wallet back into his pocket.

He didn't say anything for a second. "Tell me," looking straight at Patrick, "what do you think I should a done?" He waited. "Huh? Kill him?" He put a finger to his temple. "Bam, bam, two in the head? I'll be honest, that's what I felt like doing. But no, uh-uh, that would have been a waste. No benefit to anybody. I make a practice of recognizing opportunities. I am a businessman."

He set his palms on the table. "I believed, because I know him, that Carlos wants to be considered an honorable man, so where his mistake was concerned, he wanted to do the honorable thing, which in my books was to make amends. You give a man an opportunity to save face, you and him have an understanding, like a bond. It's a matter of respect. Carlos knows I could've turned him in, hurt him. But I didn't and he's grateful, and he rewarded me with information, a piece of this pie that's in front of us. I'm saying to you, gentlemen, don't talk to me about Carlos Parra because Carlos Parra is not here, but I am. I am running this here show. From now on if we play like I believe would be the smart thing to do, you talk to me"—his thumb hit his chest—"not him. I am the man."

Rocha looked from Oscar to Patrick and back. A long silence.

Oscar folded his arms and said, "You sound sure of yourself. That's curious, since you don't even have custody of Herman Massani. We know where he is. We have contacts at the hospital."

A smile played across Rocha's face. "Maybe I don't really want him. Maybe I'd like to get him but it's not necessary. You're forgetting I'm privy to other information," rotating his chair in Patrick's direction, "that could be damaging."

Patrick held the man's gaze. "Don't make empty threats, sir. You toss that grenade, we all get nothing."

Rocha rotated his chair away, then back. He nodded. "We can work together, Mr. Varela. And everybody will get what they want."

"Okay, you told me what you wanted, now I'd like something from you." Patrick sat forward. "In the interest of teamwork."

"My silence is not enough?" Rocha smiled.

Patrick didn't say a word.

Rocha put a hand on his chest. "What else can I possibly give you?"

"A guarantee. We businessmen need to establish a level of trust. We seek guarantees."

"You already have one. You'll get Herman Massani."

Patrick said, "Massani is not enough."

Rocha arched an eyebrow. Then he gave a sly smile and settled back in his chair, folding his hands on his stomach. He said, "Tell me. How soon do you want Freddy Robinson?"

AFTER ROCHA left, Oscar said he kept a bottle of Grey Goose in the fridge here for special occasions. He brought out two shot glasses and poured one for himself, one for Patrick. They raised their glasses, clinked, and tossed back the cold vodka.

Patrick needed it. There was a tightness in his chest, a sense of dread blooming. He suddenly wanted to be at home with his wife and kids. Doing nothing special, just to be with them.

Oscar sat, poured himself another, and took a dainty sip. Crossed his legs and appraised Patrick. "Rivera did not come through, but now we'll get both Massani and Freddy Robinson. See how things work out?"

"What about Rivera?"

"No need to worry about him talking. I couldn't get through to him on the phone I gave him, but according to one of my sources at the hospital, he's been transferred off the psych unit. To Ward D, where jail inmates go. He'll relax there, the hospital will make a report, and then after they figure he's stabilized, Rivera will be back on the street. Another patient-on-patient assault, but no charges. It's not cost-effective to bring charges against mental patients."

Patrick listened, hoping.

"Tell your brother, next time you speak to him, to follow Freddy Robinson's instructions. Time has come to turn Massani over."

Patrick nodded, his mind not fully present.

"Great. So Rocha has nothing to worry about. Now, you ever going to let me know what occurred, what this big secret is you're hiding? Seems like even Rocha knows and I don't." Oscar put a hand over his heart. "I'm hurt."

Patrick snorted, clamped his hands under his armpits, and looked at the floor. "What's the difference? Even if I wanted to tell you everything, I couldn't remember it exactly the way it happened anyway. It's so long ago, from another era. Let's forget it, Oscar."

He watched Oscar pick up his shot glass and peer into it, wearing a delicate smile. He stared back as Oscar considered him. With a salesman's silence, waiting for him to fill it.

Patrick smiled, playing cool. Problem was, he remembered it exactly the way it happened. How could he ever forget it?

13

SOMETIMES IT FELT LIKE it happened last night: Fonso driving his old pickup truck, Patrick riding shotgun and shivering from adrenaline. The loaded Glock 17 was in the glove compartment but it might as well have been on his chest, he was having such a hard time drawing a full breath. Fonso gave him a sidelong glance. "Put on some music?"

"Yeah, that'll work."

Fonso turned up the volume, Kool & the Gang's old "Celebration" bumping out of the speakers. Which didn't fit the mood of the moment, but was comfortably distracting.

On Marine Parade they slowed to pass through the narrow channel made by cars and SUVs parked outside the Radisson Fort George Hotel. Loud band music from the St. John's prom momentarily competing with the pickup's speakers. Leo was up there, drinking, probably already drunk.

They crossed the swing bridge over the river and drove down Albert Street, the Saturday night crowds strolling along the sidewalk, shops closing down. They veered right on Dean Street and parked in front of a ramshackle clapboard behind a chicken-wire-and-wood fence. Fonso tapped the horn twice. A light flashed on in a corner room and a head appeared between the thin curtains. Two minutes later the room went dark and a figure eased out of a side door and came down a short stairway.

Fonso threw an arm onto the seat back and twisted around to watch through the rear glass, a young, slender guy closing the rickety gate and hopping over the open drain, approaching the truck now. "Aw, shit," Fonso said, "since when this boy got a goatee?"

Patrick poked his head out the window to see better, pleased to have a problem to deal with, keep his mind busy.

Fonso said, "Naw, that's got to go. He need to look pretty."

Patrick watched the guy, no more than eighteen, walk up to his window. "Hello. . . . How are you . . . doing?" Halting textbook English that he probably learned at school in Guatemala.

He put a hand on the door handle, but Fonso stopped him. "Wait, Ramon. Look here"—he gestured at his own chin—"this got to go."

Ramon touched his chin, returned to the house.

Five minutes later, he was smooth-faced and they were driving in silence with the radio off, Ramon squeezed in the middle, Patrick half turned to the window. They pulled up behind a car outside the Belleview Hotel on Southern Foreshore. It was a bastard time of night, too late for the happy-hour crowd to stick around, too early for the club partiers to step out. A perfect time for an illicit liaison.

Only five cars sat parked outside the Belleview, and one of them was the Rev's Jag. Ramon went into the hotel bar while Patrick and Fonso walked across the street and down the seawall.

Soon, the Rev emerged with Ramon in tow. Patrick and Fonso moved farther down the seawall and watched the pair get into the Jag and roll south on the one-way street.

Fonso and Patrick followed them in the pickup, and when it

became clear that it was headed toward the Northern Highway, Fonso slowed down and let it pull away.

The adrenaline was surging through Patrick now and he could hear the blood in his head. The night was full of stars, a ghostly gibbous moon. For a while they were the only ones on the road. He stared into the darkness, the roadside trees an army of shadows, tires humming, sounding like it did just before he dozed off on road trips when he was a little boy. He felt his heart clutching that moment, anything to slow time, slow this truck from hurtling toward Lonesome Point and changing him for worse.

Fonso cut the lights when they came to the open gate, the truck bouncing over ruts and potholes and banking left away from the skeletons of half-finished homes, going now through the widest part of the clearing. They climbed the rise and Fonso turned the engine off on the other side, the truck coasting down to a stop.

They sat quietly, listening to their breathing. Clayey ground pale in the faint moonlight. Dark mangroves and black swampland in the distance to the left, on the right a weedy canal. Up ahead, about a hundred yards, the beach, and a single car parked there, the silver Jag.

14

L EO LAY SOAKING IN THE TUB staring up at the shampoo bottles in the shower caddy, at the small peach wall tiles, mulling over his options. His right hand held a fat joint; his left hand rested on the tub rim, two fingers in white splints. He hit the joint deep one last time, reached over and stubbed it out in the bamboo ashtray on the toilet seat. He coughed, releasing a plume.

He heard the apartment door open and Tessa say, "Uh-oh . . . smells like something's going on. . . ."

He dropped his head back and felt the high caress him, not giving a shit anymore. He heard Tessa shuffling around in the kitchen, putting groceries away. He shut his eyes and pictured her opening and closing the cabinets, big belly brushing the counter. Soon the apartment fell quiet.

When he opened his eyes, she was standing in the doorway, arms folded. Saying nothing, saying everything with her expression.

"Come in here with me," he said.

She held his gaze. "Stoned much?"

"Babe . . ." He didn't bother. He slid under, knees poking out, blew bubbles into the sudsy water, and surfaced, wiping his eyes. "You were gone a long time."

She nodded, something clearly on her mind. "I went driving. Got a few things at Publix. Should you get that wet?" indicating the stitches on his chin.

"It's all right."

She shook her head. "What's gonna happen, Lee?"

"Come here . . . come." He held his arms out. She came away from the doorway and stood at the tub, shins pressing against the side. He lifted the front of her T-shirt out and up over her belly. "Yeah, this is what I like to see." He smoothed his hands all around it, like fondling a lovely, hard balloon. "It's so beautiful. Your skin's so beautiful . . . your skin . . ."

Her eyes on his face, she said, "I went driving. Did a lot of thinking."

He leaned forward, kissed her slightly protruding navel. "It's been a long time," he whispered. Rubbing her belly, feeling dreamy.

"You know I want to. It's just gotten so uncomfortable. . . ."

With both hands holding her like a ball, he rested a cheek against her warm skin. "You're getting me all wet," she said, stooping slightly to accommodate him. He drew his head away and jiggled his eyebrows, and she slapped his arm. "Not that way. Sheeesh, you men, all the same."

She pulled away from him, moved the ashtray from the toilet lid and sat down. "I've been thinking," she said.

"You told me." He leaned back, with one hand splashed water over his chest.

"Thanks for telling me everything." She looked at him. "That *is* everything?"

"It's everything I know."

Tessa sighed. "I guess now I understand why you never talk about your parents."

He kept quiet. What was there to say? The past was like a bruise on his brain.

Tessa said, "Your mother . . . are you sure . . . how can a mother . . ." She ended by simply shaking her head.

"Like I said, Patrick told me. My mother made the decision. My father went along."

"And Freddy Robinson was the one who told you about the shooting?"

"Yeah. I call him the man who knows too much."

"How'd you suspect in the first place?"

"How could I not? I lived in the house."

"Their behavior changed?"

He thought about it. "After the Rev died, there was this . . . this fake sadness in the house. Like they thought they should act sad, they should grieve. That lasted maybe two days. After I figured things out, I thought about it, and I realized that was the weird part, they never mentioned the Rev's name."

"Your brother . . . you believe him?"

"You know, Tessa, when a person you know all your life tells you . . ." He stopped there. He'd walked this road many solitary nights and he'd found no solace, encountered no firm ground. "I believed him because I wanted to think that my brother could not be so cold-blooded. So when he told me that he couldn't do it, couldn't bring himself to pull that trigger, that it was Fonso who did it? That was fine with me because the brother I knew would never have done such a thing. I believed what I wanted to believe."

"And this story, about Fonso's deathbed confession, how Freddy said Fonso confessed to being there. You believe that?"

"He was dying of cancer. He didn't have anything to hide anymore. But all he said was, he was there. So the details . . ." Leo's fingers fluttered in the air like birds in the wind. "Who knows?"

Tessa put her elbows on her knees and rubbed her eyes. "So this is what the whole trouble is about? They hurt you like this when it's really all about your brother? Leo, you have *got* to go to the police."

"The police? And they'll do what? Haven't you heard a word I'm saying? My brother is screwed. This all comes out, it's over for him, he can kiss his career good-bye. Even if I don't care one way or the other, I don't know if this is all about him. It *seems* he's connected in some way. Hear that? *Seems.* I can't prove a thing. Go to the police? They can't protect me, Tessa. They're not bodyguards."

"So then you'll let that old man out? Leo—"

"I'm not saying that. But if I don't let him out, they might come after me again. What would be perfect, what would solve things, is if the old man was discharged. Now, that would solve my problems right there. But it's like he's been abandoned. His supposed doctor has flown the coop."

"You need to go to the police," Tessa said again, rising and walking to the door. "For me. And your baby."

Leo sank under the water, thinking and blowing bubbles. Thinking, Who would the baby resemble? Boy or girl? He wanted a girl, he had to admit. *Nadia? Melissa?* So it had come down to this? This wasn't *his* life anymore? At what hour, what minute did his worries become Tessa's, and when exactly did it become so obvious to her that his future was also hers? He surfaced to hear her say from the kitchen, "I wish you'd listen."

"Tessa?"

After a few seconds, she said, "What?"

"Can I tell you something else? About, you know, back then?"

"Hit me. Why stop now?"

"So you don't want to hear it?"

He heard the fridge closing, a cabinet creaking open. "I'm listening, Leo. First, you want your Advil with a glass of milk or no?"

"Please. Tessa?"

"Go ahead."

"Remember I said they found the Reverend in the water? Well, the police figured, from the blood trail they saw on the ground, he got shot in his car, stumbled across the beach, and fell in the water. But where was the car? Maybe I should tell you about the car."

Silence. Then, "I thought you just said you told me everything."

"I did, almost everything. There's this one last thing."

"Okay." Not sounding too sure.

"Two days after they killed the Reverend, they found his car."

"Who? Who is *they*, Leo?"

"The police. Fonso found the car."

Silence. Then, "You sound tired, Leo. You sound really tired."

He lay back against the tub. "I am."

Tessa returned with a glass of milk and two Advils. Leo stepped out of the tub and swallowed the pills with the milk and stood there dripping, holding the empty glass. She took the glass from him, tossed a towel on the floor and blotted the water, back and forth with her foot. "Go rest." Then, after a pause, "Tell me we're gonna be okay, Leo."

"We're gonna be okay, Leo."

"No, I mean it."

"We are. We are going to be okay." He wrapped a towel around his waist. "I'm gonna take a nap now, and when I wake up, no pain. Pharmaceutical magic."

She followed him into the bedroom, where he lay across the bed next to the dog Wordsworth while she stood watching him. He was sleepier than he'd thought, and the fresh sheets made him want to smile. . . .

But he couldn't sleep. His stomach was in knots. He lay still, allowing his thoughts to gel. He got up and found Tessa in the living room reading a magazine. He sat beside her. "This is what I'm going to do. I need to tell you."

She set the magazine aside.

He spoke quietly, measured. "For whatever reason, people want to harm this old man, Herman Massani. My brother knows something. I have no facts to support that. All I can say is I think that phone call telling me to keep Massani in the hospital was no coincidence. It's all twisted in my head, I can't figure it out yet. But in any case, I know Patrick, I know his ways. I also know that the best move is for the old man to be off the floor." She was about to say something, so he lifted a finger. "Wait, hold on. Not what you're thinking. I'm saying this patient needs to escape. Can't be discharged, so he'll, let's say, discharge himself. With my help."

"That's your plan."

He nodded.

"How are you going to do this, may I ask?"

"I'll tell you."

"Please do. But first, what's in it for you? Long-term, I mean. You really think these problems will go away if only Massani gets out of that stupid hospital?"

"Look at me, Tessa. I can't sleep, my stomach's a mess. I've got to do something. All my adult life, I feel like I've been running away from something. And you know what? I'll keep on running. What happened out at Lonesome Point, that's my brother's worry. He owns that one. That's *his* past. I don't even know what to believe about Patrick anymore. Let him deal with those problems. Me? I'm going to keep away from that."

"You're not like him, Lee. You don't need to keep running. You're clean, Lee, you can go to the police, you—"

"With what facts? They'll take my report, and then what? All that will do is prolong the inevitable. Two, three months later, they'll get Massani and I'll be beating myself up over the fact I could've prevented it. No, I've got a plan. First, I need the keys to the house in Wimauma. Second, pack some bags for us, get out the travel cage for the dog, 'cause we're going away and we might not be coming back."

"You can't be serious."

"Tessa, why's this so hard to believe? Tell me, what do you always say about Miami? That you want to leave here, it's so congested, crowded, people are rude, you're always complaining."

She gave a mirthless chuckle. "They don't know how to drive."

"*See?* We don't have any ties here, we can leave, start fresh somewhere else."

"That doesn't mean I'm ready to leave *now*. And where are we gonna go? And what about jobs? What're we gonna do for money?"

"Tessa, look at me," Leo turning fully to her, taking her hands. "Where have you always wanted to live? No, don't *think* about it. Tell me, from your *gut*. Be honest."

"*You* know. West coast of Florida."

He nodded. "So that's where we're going. West coast. Pick a place. There are hundreds of bars out there, restaurants, places that would hire someone like you with management experience lickety-split. And me? Hell, I'll find something, don't you worry, and believe me, it'll be better than what I have now."

She shook her head. "This is scaring me."

"It'll turn out fine. It will." He gave her hands a squeeze.

After a long while, Tessa sighed and looked him in the eyes. *Yes*.

"Don't forget your cell phone," he said. "There's a hotel in Ruskin I want you to stay at for a while. Massani's chart says he has a nephew in New Jersey. I'll reach out to him, to come down to get Massani at the farmhouse. I'll wait until five o'clock tomorrow for him. If he doesn't come by five, I'll leave Massani there. As soon as the nephew comes or I leave, whichever comes first, I'll contact you. But listen—if at five o'clock tomorrow you haven't heard from me? Call the police. Call them and tell them everything I've told you. Everything. Call them and say that the last person you saw me with was my brother."

"I don't like this."

"It's gonna be okay. I promise I'll call as soon as it's over and then, Tessa? We can go wherever you want on the west coast."

She hunched over, buried her face in her hands. When she raised her head, she said, "Don't ask me why I'm agreeing to this. When you're not the one that should be running." She reached out, held his cheek. "Your brother's the bad guy in this, not you. Why do you feel like you need to keep running? You have no reason."

He didn't want to argue. He'd made his decision, now it was time to move. He stood up, went into the bedroom and took out the clothes he wanted her to take for him and laid them on the bed. He paused. Sat down.

I don't know what to believe about Patrick anymore, he'd said. What a crock. He'd been telling himself this lie for years. He looked out the doorway, into the living room. And he sensed that Tessa knew it was a lie, too.

15

AT LONESOME POINT, Fonso and Patrick gave it a few minutes before they got out of the truck and walked across the clearing and then along the canal toward the beach. They approached the Jaguar from the rear. About fifty yards off, Fonso squatted on his haunches, signaling Patrick to do the same.

The front passenger door opened and Ramon stepped out, laughing. It was fake laughter, way too loud, and Patrick wondered if the Rev wouldn't notice. Ramon loped to the rear of the car, hands on his zipper like he was going to urinate, but he kept moving toward Fonso, hesitating when he got there. Fonso jumped up, grabbed him by the arm, and they hustled back toward the truck.

Patrick watched them vanish into the darkness. He waited a minute before he pulled the Glock from his waistband and started advancing in a crouch, slowly. So slowly. Thighs burning. An eternity between each footstep. The driver's window was closed, and now he was panicking—the glass was tinted, he wouldn't be able to see good enough to aim. . . . Why didn't he foresee this? Shit, shit. . . .

He swiveled on the balls of his feet and peered into the dark in the direction of the truck. He didn't have to go through with this. He wouldn't go through with this. No way, no how, he could not do a thing like this. His mind was racing. Fonso would have to do it. He placed the gun on the ground to get it away from his hands.

But wait, no: The window wasn't closed. Good, good, it was half open. He snatched up the gun, scooted closer, and could see inside when he straightened some. The Rev shuffling around, laying something on the seat next to him, Patrick getting closer now, pointing the gun, arm shaking. The Rev was still unaware, folding his pants on the seat, belt buckle clinking, reaching into the glove box, and the white flash of the Rev's buttocks froze Patrick.

This wasn't right, shooting a man in a compromising position like this.

He stood, watched the Rev tear open a packet with his teeth, watched him lean over and roll on a condom, and as Patrick took a step closer the Rev looked up.

Patrick lunged, pushing the barrel through the window, and the Rev screamed.

THE TRUCK windows were rolled up and bass-heavy hip-hop was pounding inside. In the light when Patrick opened the door, Ramon looked terrified.

"Let's go, let's go," Patrick said, out of breath. Ramon slid over to make room.

Fonso yanked the wheel around and drove fast for the gate, the truck bouncing through potholes, seat springs creaking as they jostled around. Once on the Northern, Fonso turned off the music and they headed back to the city in silence. Patrick's heart couldn't stop hammering, he felt nauseated and dizzy. It started to drizzle, and the asphalt turned shiny-slick in the headlights.

Fonso pulled over in front of a roadside shop. He dropped a brown envelope in Ramon's lap.

"Count it if you want."

Ramon shook his head fast and put a hand on top of the envelope like he was hiding it from someone. Patrick climbed out and stood aside for Ramon. As the boy made to leave, Fonso grabbed his arm. "Remember something for me. You don't know nothin' about nothin'."

The boy nodded.

"I want hear you say it: I don't know nothin'."

The boy shook his head. "I . . . I don't know nothing."

"Nothing about what?"

The boy started to say something but caught on and sat while Fonso stared at him.

"Just in case you forget, Ramon, I know where you live. *Entiende* me?"

Ramon looked down, nodding, getting out.

"Enjoy the money," Fonso said, and Patrick hopped in, and they left Ramon standing at the roadside.

A mile from the city, an uncontrollable trembling came over Patrick, then his teeth began to chatter. Fonso told him to take deep breaths, relax, it would pass.

Patrick inhaled deeply and blew it out with puffed-out cheeks. "You think we have anything to worry about back there, that boy?"

"Ramon?" Fonso sucked his teeth and leaned back, serene. "Shit, man, that boy so scared, if I talk too loud he'll bust out crying. Ramon ain't gonna give us no worries, trust me."

16

IT'S A SIMPLE QUESTION. People play the game all the time: If your home is on fire, what's the first thing you'd save? Leo always thought it would be his poems, the several in progress and the published ones, typeset-pretty in the handful of magazines he kept in a dresser drawer. But when Tessa took out the manila folder of yellowing loose pages and the magazines, then asked, "You want me to take these, or are you going to take them?" he was stumped.

He said, "Let me think about that a minute," and lifted yet another suitcase and carried it to the elevator. He withstood the ride down by trying not to think about anything.

Tessa's car was jam-packed with boxes, suitcases, and pillows, the big Sony television screen-down on the backseat. He popped the trunk, wedged the suitcase in beside her boxes of photo albums, which were the things that *she* always said she'd grab first in a fire.

Back upstairs, he dressed for work, rechecked his travel bag. He looked at the clock on the nightstand and stared into the deep darkness outside the window. It was almost time to leave. He walked out to the living room, to the storage closet, where Tessa was sliding out the dog's cage. Wordsworth came sniffing around. She shooed him away and looked up. "What's wrong, Leo?"

He'd planned to say something, but found himself changing his mind. "Nothing." He started for the kitchen, for a glass of water he didn't want, and turned back to her. "Need help with that?"

She was sweeping out the cage. "No, but could you check the medicine cabinet one last time?"

He walked into the bathroom. There was nothing in the cabinet he wanted. He dumped the expired bottle of Robitussin into the wastebasket, a box of Benadryl, two rusting razor cartridges. He came outside again.

After a moment, she set the broom down. "Why're you staring at me, Leo? What's wrong? You're creeping me out."

He said, "Nothing, nothing." But, yes, there was something, only he didn't know if it was the right time to say it. He went into the bedroom and stuffed the literary magazines into his bag, then, without any feeling, the folder of poems.

When they kissed good-bye at the door, her eyes were brimming. He took her hand. "I'll see you soon, okay?" He said it casually, as though what was happening later were no biggie, like they did this all the time.

She lunged at him, hugged him tight and said, "I trust you," and the unexpectedness of those words almost unmanned him, nearly caused him to drop his travel bag and pocket his keys and say, Okay, I have one more thing to tell you, but a second later that impulse lifted, and he kissed her quickly and was down the hall, turning the corner.

He passed the elevator and stopped at the garbage chute. He removed the folder of poems and considered it. He opened the chute door and chucked the folder down the chute. It felt right that he felt nothing, those poems from another place and time, an old state of mind, and the moment had come to let that go.

On the drive to work, he opened his window halfway to the breeze, remembering Tessa's question: *Why do you feel you have to keep running like this?*

BECAUSE HERE'S what happened, Tessa, he wanted to say. Here's the backstreet that brought him to this crossroad. The backstreet in Buttonwood Bay, where two nights after the Rev was killed he sat waiting in his father's car for Freddy to come out of a weed dealer's house. This is what happened: A car passed by slowly, parked two houses down. He didn't pay it much attention. It wasn't until the driver, a young Hispanic guy, a teenager it looked like, got out of the car, a silver four-door, and strode away that he was sure he recognized the car.

The Rev's stolen silver Jag.

The young guy walked into a yard and disappeared inside a house. So Leo got out of his car and strolled up for a closer look. He peeked in through the tinted driver's window, checked out the plates. There was no mistaking it: This was the Rev's.

The young guy came out of the yard, followed by a fat man with a flashlight. Leo watched them circle the Jag, talking. Starting the car. Checking under the hood; opening the trunk; opening and closing the doors. Then Leo understood. They were haggling over the price.

When Freddy came out, Leo said, "Go back inside and call Fonso. That's the Rev's car right there. Hurry."

To this day, Leo didn't know what spooked the young guy. Maybe it was Freddy running back outside after making the call, maybe he'd noticed both of them staring. But he glanced over, said something to the fat man, got into the Jag, and sped off.

The Hispanic teenager didn't know how to drive—that's the first thing Leo noticed. How in the hell do you steal a car and don't know how to drive? Freddy was cackling madly, Leo tromping the gas, Freddy saying, "You got him, yeah, yeah, cut him off now, cut him off!" But the Jag fishtailed it off the grass verge and swerved onto the Northern Highway, kicking up pebbles that bounced off Leo's windshield.

The second thing he noticed—the boy was looking for a way to bail out. His brake lights flashed on and off at every corner, the Jag slowed then sped up, slowed then sped up. Leo warned Freddy, told him to get ready for a sudden stop. A second later, the Jag swung a hard right and bulleted down a dark street on the wrong side of the road. Leo eased off the gas and took the corner, and that's when he noticed the third thing—the boy was crazy.

The Jag had slowed way down, was rolling diagonally across the street, the driver's door open, and he was getting out even as the car was still moving. Near an open drain, brake lights flashed and the boy jumped out, running. Racing through high bush, sloshing into the drain and out onto the other side and through an empty lot, going for a backyard.

Leo stopped the car and he and Freddy scrambled out after him. Leo tripped over something and flew forward onto the street. But he leaped up and continued running, and the question he still had, after all these years, was why didn't he take that fall as a sign? Why didn't he stop to brush off his hands, take a deep breath, and just think? Turn back, get in his car, drive away? But he didn't, he wanted to tell Tessa now, he was clueless then, he never thought for one second that this boy was not some random car thief, and so he kept up the chase, getting himself involved in affairs darker than his foolish young self ever could imagine.

THE

CHASE

BOOK II

17

THE PSYCH WARD WAS A MADHOUSE. That's what Leo would tell Tessa sometimes when she asked how his night had been. Well, tonight the description was apt every which way, and it really wasn't funny.

A new patient in a wheelchair in Room 316 yelled constantly for help to go to the bathroom, Rafael in 310 had landed in seclusion after flinging his dinner tray at a nurse, Dolores Washburn had been wailing up and down the hall when Leo punched in, and one hour later she hadn't stopped, and the TV room reeked of piss and disinfectant.

Leo went about his work and tried to let the stress roll off him. He escorted Dolores to bed and knocked off the hallway lights on the women's side. After that, he kept to himself. When Martin asked, Leo said he'd broken his fingers taking a spill on the basketball court. Martin seemed to believe it.

The biggest news of the night: Reynaldo Rivera had been transferred to Ward D. He could expect to be there a long while, Rose said, Dr. Burton was in no rush to discharge him. Leo wanted to know where was he going after that. Back on the streets? Rose told Leo he got it right in one try. Leo left the room with the rounds board, shaking his head, worry darkening his mood.

Rose had given him last break. No matter, he'd get tonight's mission accomplished one way or another. He went to Massani's room and poked his head in. The old man sat awake in a chair staring out the window. *"Quién es?* Who is that?"

Leo opened the door wide so the hallway light poured in. "It's me, Herman. Can't sleep?"

Herman sat up stiffly, hands gripping the armrest. He was scared.

If his plan was going to work, he'd have to put Herman at ease, and he didn't have long. Moving carefully, he sat on the edge of the bed across from Herman. "Hey," he said in a level tone, "I want you to know that as long as I'm here, nothing's gonna happen to you. Okay, Herman?"

The old man pulled a blanket around his bony shoulders and looked out the window. "They want to kill me."

"I know, Herman. I know. That's why I'm gonna help you."

The old man kept staring out the window, lights burning in the windows of the building across the courtyard. "I don't know who you are."

Leo said it softly. "I'm the man who saved you this morning."

The old man pulled the blanket tighter around himself. He wiggled his toes and studied them for a bit. "Who are you? What is your name?"

"My name is Leo."

"Habla español?"

"The answer is the same as the last time you asked me."

"I see you writing out there sometimes. You are a policeman? Detective, under the cover?"

"No, nothing like that. I work here."

"What are you writing?"

Leo set the clipboard on the bed. *"Trying* to write. Poems."

The old man looked at him quizzically. "Poetry?" He contemplated this a moment. Turning to the window he said, almost whispering, *"Puedo escribir los versos mas tristes esta noche."*

Which made Leo smile. "Neruda. 'Tonight I can write the saddest lines.' "

Herman nodded. " *'El viento de la noche gira en el cielo y canta.'* "

Leo said the line in English: " 'The night wind revolves in the sky and sings.' "

For the first time he could remember, he saw the old man smile. Okay, so this was a fortunate little development, but he couldn't rush it. He said, "And then there's that line, says that he loved her and sometimes she loved him too."

Herman said, "Maybe that is the best we can hope for? They will return your love— but only sometimes?" He nodded again. "Neruda."

"One of the masters, if you ask me."

"So why do you want to help me, poet? How much do you want for this?"

Leo said, "Just hold on there. Before you think I'm trying to shake you down, let me hit you with a dose of reality. Have you spoken to your doctor recently?"

"You talked to the nurses, eh? They told you I was calling Dr. Garrido."

"You tried all day, didn't you, and no luck. Tell me something, Herman. Is Garrido the one who was going to arrange a place for you to stay when you left here?"

Herman said, "I need to get out of here. It's not safe for me here no more."

Leo got up, shut the door, snapped on the light so Herman could see his face, and returned to his seat on the bed. "Listen to me, now. I am not here to shake you down in any way, but I want you to know you're in bigger trouble than you think. I don't know why people are looking for you but they are, and Dr. Garrido won't be around to help you this time. Listen up," and Leo told him about the doctor's abandoned office in Hialeah and the two men who were waiting around for Garrido to show, and it sure as hell wasn't for their health's sake, or the doctor's, he said. "The only savior you got right now is me, Herman. I don't want your money, okay? I just need you to hear what I'm saying and for you to trust me if you want to make it outta here."

He showed Herman his broken fingers. "Look at what they did to me this morning because I refused to hand you over to them. So you've got to believe me that no one's gonna hurt you if I can prevent it, and they sure as shit ain't going to hurt me again as long as I'm healthy enough to run and hide and out-smart their asses. But I need you to trust me, and we'll be all right. You think you can do that? You don't have much time to think it over, though, because we have to leave this place to-night."

Herman struggled to his feet; you could almost hear his bones creaking. He stared at Leo. "Tonight? So you are a detective who is a poet who don't know me and wants to help me for a reason I don't know why?"

Leo glanced at his watch, scratched his jaw. "Herman, I didn't want to tell you this just yet but, you know, maybe it's better so you'll understand I'm not hiding anything from you. My name is Leo Varela. That last name rings a bell?"

"Varela?" Herman shuffled toward him and peered into his eyes. "Commissioner Varela? He is your family?"

"My brother. Did you ever work for him or have dealings with anyone associated with him, anything like that?"

"I-ya-yie," Herman said, clapping a hand over his chest, *"Dios mio* . . . my heart is flying out of my body. Go ahead, tell your brother, go, you win," waving Leo away without looking at him.

Leo jumped up. "Hold on there, now. Listen to me, okay? I don't work for him. I'm an eleven-dollars-an-hour mental health tech in a hospital for indigents and you happened to walk in here and now people who I don't know come telling me to walk you out, or else my brother, the politician, is gonna pay. That's it, that's my predicament. I don't know anything else about what's going on, what scheme this is." His voice had risen, so he stopped himself and said, softly now, "I'm being up front with you. I could leave you here and it'll be a matter of time before they get to you. Or you could trust me and with my help get the hell out and find someplace to hide. It's your choice."

"Why are you doing this? Helping me?"

"Because it's the right thing to do. I'm doing this for me. Trust me when I tell you that."

Herman went to the window and shrugged the blanket off his shoulders. He looked out across the courtyard, not speaking for the longest time, and Leo thought he was crying. Leo approached, thought he heard sobbing but wasn't sure. He lifted the blanket and spread it over Herman's frail shoulders. Herman reached up, clamped a hand over Leo's. After a moment, he nodded.

"*Ayudame, por favor.*"

THE WARD was quiet at last, and how the rest of the night was going to play out depended a lot on Leo's mind-set. So walking toward the nurses' station, he was working on slow, gentle breathing. Shake the tension from your shoulders, relax your jaw muscles. He and Herman had had the talk and from here on it was about actions, no doubts, no second-guessing.

Rose was at the computer, Martin at the far side of the room doing paperwork. An abnormal silence hung in the air. Rose would check off a box on a form, sign it, and set the form aside instead of sliding it across the desk for Martin to file. Martin had to get up to reach it. If it was Leo doing the filing, then her inconsiderate behavior would be expected, but with Martin? No, something wasn't right.

Leo busied himself replenishing patients' charts with forms. He sat listening to the paper-shuffling, keyboard clicking under Rose's long red fingernails, Martin occasionally clearing his throat. The ringing phone jolted him and he grabbed it, knowing who it was before he even looked at the caller ID. "Jefferson Memorial, Annex Three, may I help you?"

"Evening, Leo," Patrick said. "Sorry I didn't call you earlier."

"Hey." Leo easing back in his seat, tight smile on his face, bracing for the lies.

"It's been a helluva busy day for me. And I thought now would be a better time to speak with you anyway." A pause. "Listen, about our patient. We need to get this situation resolved. I've been doing some thinking, spoke to my campaign adviser, and we determined: This thing is no threat to me. Freddy Robinson's people want this patient? Let them have him."

"Wow." Leo unable to rein in the sarcasm. "This is a complete one-eighty shift for you."

"I know that, but Freddy has nothing on me. I'd slap him with a defamation-of-character suit so fast it would wipe his memory clean."

"Just a coupla days ago you said—"

"I know what I said then, but are you understanding what I'm telling you now?"

Leo stood and walked outside the room, stretching the cord around the corner. Keeping his voice down, he said, "Well, the man, Mr. M., was attacked last night. Didn't you hear?"

"How would I have heard about that?"

"Yeah, well, he was assaulted by another patient and was hurt. He's not doing too good. He's . . . he's in bed, actually, nurses checking him 'round the clock. I'm kinda surprised, to tell you the truth, he wasn't transferred to the medical side."

After a few seconds, Patrick said, "So what are you telling me?"

Leo leaned against the wall. "Tonight might not be the best night for a move but if we do it, we've got to change the hour."

Patrick breathed hard into the phone. "And when would be a better hour?"

Leo glanced down both sides of the empty hallway. "Judging from how this place is unusually busy at the moment, I plan to tell Freddy we shoot for four-thirty, the place is really quiet then. Maybe even five."

"But it'll be tonight."

"Yes." Leo held the phone tight. "Patrick, they broke my fingers. They broke my fucking fingers, man."

"*What . . . ?* Who?"

"One of Freddy's thugs."

"Christ, are you all right?"

"I am *now*. Hurt like hell when it happened, but I'll survive. You know why they did it, right?"

"I know, I know. I'm sorry. I owe you big time."

"Patrick. What's going on? I need to know."

"What's going on? I'll be damned if I know, Leo, really."

"Bullshit."

"Hey, now, you gotta believe me. Don't do this, don't turn on me in the middle of the game. Let's get this show over with, Leo. I'll find out what this is all about, I will. Then we'll talk. They're not gonna get away with this shit, I promise you that, but just don't back out on me now."

"Who is this old man Massani? You have any idea?"

There was a silence. "Leo. Buddy. I'll find out. I will. Now help me. Them hurting you like this? This is getting way, way outta hand. Let's turn him over tonight and put this shit behind us. Freddy's day will come, believe you me. Can you do it tonight? Come on, buddy."

Leo said, "Yeah, I can do it," thinking how he must look like a fool to Patrick. Thinking, We'll see soon who the fool is in this game, Patrick.

"Call me when it's over. Anytime. I probably won't get much sleep anyway."

Leo said, "Okay," thinking that this might be one of the last times he spoke to his brother. And how did he feel about that? He felt empty. "One last thing, one question I have. Why'd you tell me not to let him out last night?"

"Look, I was being cautious. I consulted with my adviser, my staff, and we thought we needed to know more about who Freddy Robinson is working for before we just, well, reacted. We needed to arrive at a smart, informed response."

"Is that what we're doing now?"

"I'd say so. Let's end this tonight, Leo. I'm not putting my career or your safety on the line anymore."

Ever the politician.

Leo said, "I understand." Only too well.

"Good, Leo. When it's over, when this all goes away, we'll have to go out, have dinner together, just me and you. Let me make it up to you."

AFTER THE call, Leo felt on edge and needed to walk it off. He grabbed the rounds board and headed down the darkened hallway, turned at the door, and started back. All the patients safely in their rooms on the women's side, one patient in the bathroom on the men's. He'd spied a figure shuffling in but it was too dark to make out the person. He waited near the door for the man to exit to see who it was. Frankie, the masturbator from Room 318, emerged wiping his hands on his pajama pants and reared back. "Jesus Christ!"

"Sorry, Frankie. Didn't mean to scare you."

Frankie had backed up, palms flat on the door, eyes huge.

"Hey, it's me. Leo. What's wrong with you? It's all right, now. Come, let's go back to your room."

"I needed to take a shit."

"Good for you. You're allowed. Let's go, now."

"It was a good shit. A healthy shit."

"Hurray." Leo led Frankie to his room door. "You have a good night, okay?"

"I'll try. I been trying but all the rats in there keeping me awake, thumping and bumping and jumping."

"Rats, huh?" Leo frowned with feigned thoughtfulness. This was like a dozen other conversations he'd had over the years with patients who had been spitting out meds on the sly or who needed dosages increased. "Let's go inside, see if we can find any of these rats, then."

Leo tapped on the room light. Two beds, no sheets on one because Frankie's roommate, Reynaldo Rivera, had been transferred. Just thinking about that man chilled Leo to his stomach. He stood in the middle of the room, between the two beds. "You're keeping your room nice and clean, Frankie. I'm looking around here and, man, I can't see no rats. You see any?"

Frankie pointed to the ceiling. "They up there. I hear them."

Leo pointed to the ceiling. "Up there."

"Uh-huh."

"I assure you, you don't have rats in your ceiling, but just to be sure, I tell you what I'll do. I'll make a note and when the exterminator's here next time we'll get him on it first thing, how's that sound?"

"Good. Then maybe I'll get some sleep." Frankie pulled back his sheets and climbed in.

"Good night, Frankie." Leo hit the lights. He walked back to the nurses' station thinking, Thumping, bumping rats, yeah, right. Frankie probably knew well enough he was being humored but how else to respond to a complaint like that? The phone in the nurses' station was ringing and he heard Martin say, "Hello, Annex Three," and Leo stopped and turned around and looked down toward Frankie's room.

Could it be? Yesterday Dolores, the patient, had told him she'd seen Reynaldo with a cell phone. When patients hid phones in their rooms, what did they do to keep them from being confiscated? Put them on vibrate.

He strode back, opened Frankie's door, and said, "Sorry to bug you so soon but the exterminator's here." He put on the lights and Frankie sat up in bed. Leo closed the door and set the rounds board on the dresser. "Where'd you say the rats were hiding? About here?" Pointing to the ceiling above Reynaldo Rivera's old bed. Frankie nodded.

Leo heeled off his shoes and stood on the bed. He reached up with both hands, pushed up a ceiling panel. It gave easily. Fiber dust dropped into his eyes and he stopped to wipe them with his shoulder sleeves. He stood on tiptoe and peered into the ceiling space, couldn't see a damn thing. He reached a hand and felt around. His fingers brushed something solid. He took a latex glove from his pocket, pulled it on. Holding up the panel with one hand, he stretched his gloved hand as far as he could, and right . . . there . . . got it. His hand came down grasping a silver cell phone.

Frankie craned his neck. "What's that there?"

"A big rat." Leo flipped the phone open. Time and date accurate, two bars of power left. He went into the Names option: blank. He pressed the Menu option and selected Call History and scrolled through outgoing and incoming and missed calls. All incoming calls were from one number. All outoing calls, the same. Missed calls, ditto.

The phone was there to serve one purpose. Leo felt his neck tensing. He thumbed off the phone's power. Pushed the phone into a pants pocket, replaced the ceiling panel, and hopped off the bed.

He put on his shoes and said to Frankie, "The rat is officially dead. Sleep tight, now." He flipped the lights off and walked out.

Back in the nurses' station, the cold war between Martin and Rose was continuing. When he dropped the rounds board on the wall hook with a deliberate clatter, they hardly looked up. He cleared his throat. Martin smiled thinly at him, then went back to his paperwork. Leo thought, Good, and left.

When he returned to Herman's room, the old man was still awake, sitting by the window in the darkness, blanket around his shoulders, tennis shoes on. He rose halfway. "Ready? *Estoy listo.*" A drawstring plastic bag stuffed with clothes sat in his lap.

"Not yet," Leo said. He took a seat on the bed. "Herman, I have a phone number to ask about," and he recited the number. "You familiar with it, by any chance?"

"But of course."

Leo waited.

"You mean you don't know whose number it is?"

"Tell me."

"That number, *es de tu hermano.*"

"My brother's? That's not my brother's number."

"Yes. Is the number for the campaign manager, the adviser. Señor Oscar."

Leo sat up and took a deep breath. He'd been having doubts; he'd been telling himself, No second-guessing, but he'd been having misgivings about tonight. Because this was his brother, his *blood*, and what could Leo really prove? But Herman had just helped him refocus. The firm connection between Patrick and the man who had tried to kill Herman was this phone right here in his pocket.

MARTIN SAW him coming out of Herman's room. Leo pretended to be too busy closing the door to notice. Martin met him halfway down the hall. "Everything fine with the old guy?"

Leo walked toward him. "A bit shaken up, but he'll be okay."

Martin fidgeted with his watch. "Hey, you want to put together some extra patients' charts with me tonight?"

Leo said he could do that, just let him grab something to drink and get some progress notes squared away. Still putting on the busy act. Martin said sure, no rush, but he followed him down the hall and stood there scratching an ear while Leo opened the kitchen door with a key. Inside, Leo got a plastic container of apple juice from the fridge and leaned against the counter, watching Martin standing there by the door, looking awkward.

"Something on your mind, Martin?"

The young man adjusted his watchband, buried both hands in his pockets. "Hey, you know Rose and I, well, we're kinda dating?"

Leo nodded, gestured for him to continue.

"Well, I heard that you and she kinda dated way back, and, uh, I don't know, so I was thinking you might know her better?"

Leo sipped his juice. "What're you asking me?"

Martin cleared his throat, shifted his feet, eyes on the floor. "For advice? You went out with her, you know her. Before she broke up with you, was she ever moody or, like, temperamental?"

Broke up with you? Leo wanted to say, Actually, we went on two dates, which in hindsight were completely uncalled-for. He was about to ask Martin if she was the one who'd handed him this version when it occurred to him that an opportunity had just appeared. Stay on your toes, Lee, that's right, stay alert. So he sidled up to Martin. Put a hand on his shoulder. "She's giving you a hard time already, huh? Blowing something minor way out of proportion, I bet?"

Martin gazed at him, looking childlike. "Yes, exactly, it's ridiculous. We were at Shoney's and I was just being nice to the waitress and, man—"

"Listen, listen," Leo nodding, giving the guy's shoulder a squeeze, "it's all right, it's all right. It's not your fault," a part of him suddenly wanting to laugh at his own bullshit. "That's how she is—but there's a way." He lifted a finger, gaining control over himself.

"A way?"

Leo nodded. "Yes," keeping the finger raised, then pointing to Martin's chest. "You have the power to change the course of the relationship. You can change it"—he snapped his fingers—"like that."

"You think so?"

Leo stayed quiet.

Martin said, "Why's that?"

Leo knew this wouldn't work with someone older or more experienced than Martin, so he forged on, like he was stating the obvious: "Because of who she is, Martin, the kind of woman Rose is."

"What do you mean?"

Leo sighed. Put a hand on Martin's shoulder, commiserating with the fellow. "She's complicated, isn't she? Sweet one minute, demanding the next. But the one thing, the one constant— she likes, no: she *needs* your attention. No half measures for Rose, that's what I learned." Leo's hand fell away from Martin's shoulder and he gazed wistfully into the middle distance, like a lover overcome by sad memories. At the same time, he was trying hard to force out of his head the images of the graffiti Rose had sprayed on his car when he'd backed out of the relationship: *Worthless user!* He said to Martin, "If you like her, Martin, and I think you do—show her. Give her a pleasant surprise. I think she'd cherish that. You should do it tonight."

"Tonight? How?"

Leo picked up his juice and drank, taking his time for dramatic effect. "Rose goes on break in a few minutes, am I right? So here's what you can do. It's romantic and spontaneous, and she'll love it." He leaned in, dropped his voice. "When she goes into the conference room, give her about five minutes after she closes that door, time to pull out the bed and spread the linen. Then you go and you knock on the door. Firmly."

Martin made a face. "Oh, I don't know if I want to do that, you know, it's—"

"No, wait." Leo set a hand gently on Martin's forearm. "It's not exactly what you're thinking. This is about the *suggestion*, the *show* of taking control. Listen, she'll say, 'Who is it?' or she might even open the door, and what you do, you stand right there, act cool and composed, and you say, 'Rose, I need to speak to you for a moment, please. There is something I'd like to say.' And then you keep quiet and just wait for her response. If she says something like, 'Can't it wait?' you say, real cool, 'No, it can't, I'm afraid,' and something like how now is as good a time as any, and then you say, 'Rose, I want to come in.' You don't ask, you *tell* her you want to go inside, and you keep looking her straight in the eyes, Martin, and don't you doubt for a second that she'll let you in."

The young man was thinking it over, squeezing his bottom lip. "But why do I want to do all this?"

"Demonstrate to her she's on your mind, and it can't wait anymore and you've got to talk to her, and like right now."

Martin nodded, warming to the plan.

"Lemme tell you," Leo said, deciding to nudge things three degrees, "with that room dark, that bed laid out, it's the perfect setting, the ambience for an intimate conversation. A heart-to-heart. I'll cover for you on the floor, there's nothing to worry about. After you do it? Talk to her, I mean? You'll feel a lot better about where you guys stand, and she will, too. Tonight's a perfect time."

Martin let out a sigh. He stared at the counter, maybe picturing how it would go. "All right," he said. "Why the heck not? You'll cover for me?"

"Of course. Don't worry about a thing, dude."

AT 1:45, the phone rang and Rose, who was getting ready for her break, picked up. Leo was sitting in the gerri chair in the hallway. Rose sauntered past him with a pillow and a blanket and said, "It's for you."

Leo took the call.

Freddy Robinson said, "Four o'clock. You know what you have to do."

"Wait. . . ." Leo sat down. "A little later is a better time because of the break situation." Martin walked into the room, and Leo hunched over the phone for privacy.

"Gimme a set hour, man," Freddy said.

"Okay, I'm thinking four-thirty."

"Then I shall see you and Mr. Massani at four-thirty."

And Freddy hung up.

Leo returned to the gerri chair with butterflies in his stomach. He tried to think through his plan one more time, but for a long freaky moment his mind was blank. He shook his head, sat up straight and exhaled, and the gears started working again. His hands had gone cold, so he rubbed them together, put some feeling back. All right, he was too nervous, he needed to cool it. He tapped his toes.

At 1:54, Martin left the nurses' station, nodded at Leo and trekked down the hall toward the break room. Leo watched, three people on his mind: Martin, Freddy, Herman. Leo could make out Martin's form in the darkness as he rapped on the break-room door and stood back. The door opened, there was some murmuring, Martin walked in, and the door closed. Leo jumped up and walked to the door. When he heard the lock engage, he made his move.

He closed the nurses' station, only a small square of light spilling into the hall now from the glass in the door. He checked his pockets, car keys and wallet there, plus his pocketknife, just in case. All that was left was Herman.

In his room, Herman was ready—baggy khaki pants and a red polo shirt, white tennis shoes without laces—holding his drawstring plastic bag of clothes. *"Ahora?"*

"That's right, *ahora.*"

Leo hustled the old man down the hall past the locked break room, where—he was positive, would bet his last dollar—Martin and Rose were deep into it. Because if there was one thing Leo had learned in two dates with her—the woman had emotional issues, confused sex with commitment, and required you to prove, with lots of sweat and exertion, how deeply committed you were. May the good Lord give Martin stamina.

They hurried past the nurses' station now and all the doors of the women's side, lights off in all the open rooms, the ward quiet except for Herman's loose sneakers slapping the tiles.

Leo opened the back door with a key and they stepped out into the warm stairwell. They trudged down a flight of stairs before Leo stopped. "Look, you don't have laces? We'll need to move fast, and those things'll fly right off and you'll be running barefoot."

Herman shook his head. Leo shook his head, too. "Come on," and they continued until they reached the bottom of the stairs and Leo said, "Get behind me." He cracked the door just enough to view the parking lot, air cooling his face. He'd parked his car in a middle row near the fence, a straight shot from the door, and as far as he could see nobody was lurking there.

But Leo knew better. He knew Freddy didn't trust him, and that's why Freddy was about to get tricked. He told the old man, "Let's go, hurry."

Roughly halfway to his car, he threw a glance to his right. Across the street in the lit-up short-term lot, Freddy was leaning against a car, arms folded, grinning at them. Then Leo saw a movement up ahead on the left: Bernard stepping out of the black Mercedes. Welcome, Bernard.

Leo grabbed Herman's arm and directed him back to the annex, toward the courtyard gate. Fumbling with the keys to find the right one, trying to do it coolly so as not to frighten Herman.

Bernard hollered, "Yo!"

Leo slipped in the gate key, Herman conscious of the situation now and turning around.

"Hold up there!"

Leo pushed open the gate, hauled the old man in, slammed the gate shut.

Bernard shouted something incoherent, shoes clacking as he came running.

Herman dropped his bag, Leo swiped it up and kept tugging Herman along as they race-walked under the basketball hoop and across the courtyard. He heard Bernard rattling the gate, shouting, "What game you playing, boy? You fixing to get your head lumped!"

At the south side of the courtyard, Leo opened a door with a key, and they entered a hallway, administration offices on both sides, doors closed. They headed toward the door at the end, a security camera in a corner above it, Leo knowing that guards would be on his ass in minutes. He paused in front of the camera, made sure they got a good look at him and Herman. Then he pushed through the door, into the lobby of the pharmacy, the two of them breathing noisily under the bright fluorescent lights. A hallway in front led to the rest of the hospital, a hallway to the left led to Crisis, sliding glass doors to the right.

Leo said, "You okay?"

Herman's skin was flushed. He nodded, managing a weak smile.

"We're taking these," Leo said, pointing at the sliding doors, "out to the parking lot again, but going in the other direction. If we see that big guy again, if you feel me grab you hard again, like this, we're heading back, understand?"

Herman nodded and Leo smiled for encouragement when a security guard in a blue jacket marched up the hallway, carrying a radio. Beautiful, these guys were good. Leo dug out his hospital ID badge from a pocket. The guard's radio crackled. He raised it to his mouth, spoke, glaring at Leo and Herman when he reached them.

"You gentlemen work here?" His eyes swept over Herman's bag with the Jefferson Memorial logo, the tennis shoes with no laces.

Leo presented his ID. "Upstairs, mental health."

The guard examined the ID, looked at Leo, handed it back. "What were you doing in Administration, Mr. Varela?"

"Well, this patient here, he was . . ." He saw the guard glance to the left.

Big Bernard was strolling down the hallway from Crisis.

Leo said, "That's the guy."

The guard said, "What guy?"

"That's what I'm saying, that's why we sneaked into Administration. That's the dude was chasing my patient I took down to Crisis for a checkup and he's screaming at Herman here and getting him all agitated, I don't know what the hell's going on, where were you guys?"

The guard looked at Herman, Herman nodding at him. The guard turned and walked toward Bernard. He spoke into his radio, and Bernard slowed his advance, then stopped.

Leo took Herman's arm and edged toward the sliding doors.

The guard reached Bernard and began talking to him, Bernard staring at them over the man's shoulder. Another guard was coming up behind Bernard, who heard and turned around.

Leo said quietly, "Let's go," and he gripped Herman harder and they took off, trotting through the doors. One of Herman's shoes slipped off in the parking lot and he bent over to get it as they were moving and went sprawling onto his stomach. Jesus Christ. Leo hoisted him up and they started off again, leaving the shoe behind.

Leo saw Freddy, off in the distance, perched on the trunk of Leo's car like a man with no worries. Leo stuck close to the building, dragging Herman and thinking this was what life amounted to, running around in circles searching for a way out of this bullshit at two o'clock in the morning. They hit the sidewalk and turned the southwest corner of the building.

Herman was panting, asking where were they going, he was tired, he couldn't . . . Leo told him it was almost over, not much farther, then, holding Herman's hand like a child's, he crossed the hospital campus's main road, across the cobblestone plaza with the fountain, heading for the four-story parking garage.

18

THE GATE ARM ROSE and the old blue Camry rolled out of the garage onto the main campus road, Tessa behind the wheel, nervous and fidgety. She looked left, looked right, and for a second was confused. Which way led out?

She chose left, going extra slow when all she really wanted to do was speed, zoom, fly the hell out of there. But no, she needed to play this game right, not attract attention. Even though there was nobody on the road, and that's exactly what was unnerving her—the place too quiet, pretty flower beds there by the benches, water splashing in the fountain she was passing now, the tires bump-bump-bumping over the cobblestone. Everything was a little too peaceful.

At the bend in the road, the headlights swept over the mental health annex and the parking lot and then she saw the main entrance and felt a lift. She pressed the pedal a touch harder. When she was almost there, she saw a man in the parking lot, a slim black guy in a tie standing around like he was waiting for a bus.

At the main gate the traffic light blinked yellow. She stopped, looked both ways on Twelfth Avenue, again fighting the urge to mash the pedal.

A huge man appeared from behind the fence and stepped in front of the car. Tessa gasped, couldn't help it.

The man grinned at her. Not moving. A huge head, perfectly

round and smooth. He was nicely dressed, tie and long-sleeve shirt. Raised a small flashlight in his fist, like cops do, spotlighting her.

Tessa shielded her eyes, rolled down a window, the man coming around to her side, lowering the beam but his eyes never leaving her face. Tessa said, "Officer, Officer, thank god, I'm so lost."

"Yo, lady, I'm not—"

"I need to get to the emergency room, I'm having awful pains." Tessa touched her belly. "Just awful and I'm not due for a couple months and I need to see a doctor quick but I'm just so lost."

"The emergency room is on Tenth Avenue. You go down this street, Twelfth right here, take the first right, then a right onto Ninth and down a ways to Eighteenth, and you see the sign for it there on the right."

"A right here, two more rights . . . oh, thank you so much."

Tessa was about to take her foot off the brake when the man said, "Wait," and moved close to the window and shone the light into the backseat. An overnight bag, a pile of blankets on the floor.

Tessa said, "Oh, this hurts. . . ."

The man stepped back. "Sorry." Clicked off the beam.

"Thank you, Officer."

"It's all right, but I'm not—"

Tessa rolled up the window and roared off, banking right and racing up Twelfth Avenue. She ripped through the intersection where she was supposed to turn right, then said, "Okay, who was that, who the hell was that?"

Blankets flew up into the air and landed next to her, and Leo rose up and spilled onto the backseat, breathing heavily. "That was close . . . that was too close."

"Who was that, Leo?"

He wiped perspiration off his face with his sleeve and climbed into the front seat. "Bernard. His name's Bernard." Leo raised the splints. "He's the one. Pull over, babe, pull over and pop the trunk."

Tessa aimed for a warehouse parking lot, the car careening over the curb and lurching to a halt. Leo jumped out and ran around to the trunk. Herman lay curled up inside, hugging his bag and one shoe. Leo helped him out and hustled him into the backseat. "If I wasn't claustrophobic I'd have gotten in there, Herman, I swear, but you did good. Lie down flat now, don't raise your head." Then Leo hopped back into the front seat. "Go go go."

Tessa peeled out onto Twelfth again and tore north through the blinking yellow lights of empty intersections and down a maze of dark streets toward I-95. After everyone seemed to calm down, after her heart had slowed, it all began to sink in. "I can't *believe* we're doing this," she said. "I can't believe I let you talk me into this."

"Tessa, this is Herman. Herman, this is my fiancée, Tessa."

She threw the old man a backward glance. "Hi, nice to meet you." She looked at Leo. "I'm never doing anything like this again, so don't ever ask me."

"Okay. But do you love me?"

"Your chin's bleeding."

He touched it.

"Don't, your hands are dirty."

"I must've hit myself on the floor just now and didn't even realize."

"Let me see. Come here, let me see."

"You're driving." But he obeyed anyway, leaning toward her.

"It's your stitches, all right. You might want to clean it. When we stop at the apartment you should come up, I'll wash it."

"We don't have time. Watch the road, Tess."

"That needs cleaning, though."

"Sure, but do you love me?"

Herman was sitting up. "The ramp. For the highway. Is here now."

"Oh, shit." Tessa jerked the wheel to the left, sweeping past a blare of horns and oncoming traffic and up the ramp to I-95.

Leo looked shocked. "Now, that was unnecessary."

"Shut up." She rolled her window down and increased the speed. "I think I have some names. If it's a boy, Dominic. If it's a girl, Jolene."

"You're thinking of names at a time . . . *Dominic?* You're kidding, right? Dominic?"

"What's wrong with that?"

Herman said, "Dominic is a nice name."

Leo said, "Huh?" He looked back at the old man and then at Tessa and started to smile.

"I love you," she said. "And I want us to be safe. Should I ask you to promise you'll come back safe?"

"I promise I'll do my best. Promise you won't worry?"

"Can't promise that."

He nodded, looked out the window. "I'll call Herman's nephew in New Jersey as soon as we're on the road. Soon as he comes for

Herman, I'll call you. Don't forget your cell phone, and just be ready."

"And after that?"

He chewed the inside of his cheek. "After that, Miami will be where we *used* to live." He squeezed her hand, she squeezed back. "Go faster, Tess, the road is all yours."

19

H OW IS THAT POSSIBLE?" Patrick sat down in the leather chair of his home office, holding the phone to his ear. "He walked out of the hospital and disappeared into the ether, is that what you're telling me?" He rocked back and forth, finger-raked his hair, and listened. He said, "Jesus Christ. I have no idea what my brother thinks he's doing . . . I really don't." He stood up, looked out the window at Biscayne Bay and listened to Oscar's bad news.

When he put the phone down and turned around, Celina was standing in the doorway. He didn't know how long she'd been there. "Celina . . ."

"I came to ask would you like a cup of tea."

He arranged some papers on his desk, slipped them into an envelope. "That would be nice, actually."

She nodded. Staring at him.

He said, "Celina?" but she was already walking away.

In the kitchen he stood at the island while she poured water from the kettle into two cups with tea bags, set out the sugar bowl, a container of Half & Half. He watched her stir, the clink of spoon against cup sounding amplified.

She took a sip. "I like having you home. Just talking to you here, middle of the week like this, the kids at school. No interruptions, so we can have a decent conversation."

"I know what you mean."

"You're hardly here enough to enjoy your home," she said, gesturing at the granite counters, the glass-front cabinets with wine rack. "You haven't made shrimp scampi in the longest. It's you who wanted that professional stove over there. Know something? We haven't sat down, just us two, and enjoyed a meal and a bottle of wine, just talk, in an eternity." She canted her head. "Can I tell you something else?"

"You've already started."

"We're growing apart. No. I mean it. We have this," and she tossed a hand to the floor-to-ceiling window views of the bay, "but we're losing each other."

"I know what you're saying, I know. Celina, listen, this campaign, it's been much more difficult than I expected."

"Will you stop?" She folded her arms. "Patrick, do you think I know you?"

He nodded and looked down at his cup.

"Of course I do. So don't tell me it's the campaign and think I'll just accept that. Something's been troubling you, something besides your campaign. I don't know what it is but I want you to tell me. Do you hear me, Patrick?"

He tilted his head toward his office. "You thought you overheard something when I was on the phone?"

"I've known you for fifteen years, Patrick. I can see the truth all over your face. Remember those tough days after you started your own firm? Who knew right away there was something wrong? *I* did. Just like I know there's something wrong now. Only now you're not alone in this. And I will not—do you hear?—I will *not* stand for me and the kids going down this road blindly with you. I'm not putting up with your evasions."

He studied her, sipped his tea. "You won't let this go, will you?" Trying to sound dismissive but at the same time admiring her toughness.

"As long as we're in this house together, you bet I won't. If whatever is happening here ends up hurting me or the kids, I will pack your bags and leave them by the door and my lawyer'll be calling you faster than you can say alimony. Or you can speak to me now and let me help you."

Patrick looked at her for a long time before he plodded over to the breakfast nook with his tea. He looked out the window, nodding to himself. "Okay, Celina. You want to know, so here it is."

She sat down across from him.

"It's Leo," he said. "He's causing me some grief. He took this man, a guy we've been looking for, involved with the campaign, out of the hospital, the psych ward there, and we've lost track of them."

Celina raised her chin, closed her eyes briefly. "Wait." She moved her cup out of the way and reached across the table, taking his hand. "Begin from the beginning, my love."

LEO WHEELED the Camry into a Chevron station just off I-75 in Sarasota. Herman was wearing an old ball cap Leo had pulled from the overnight bag in the backseat, and Leo was sporting a bandage on his chin that Tessa had plastered on when they'd dropped her off at the apartment. That had been three hours ago. The morning had turned hot and bright and for the first time since they fled the hospital, Leo allowed himself to feel optimistic. Just a little.

He bought two cups of coffee, cheap scissors and even cheaper sunglasses, and ten bucks' worth of gas out of habit. He passed a cup to Herman, slouched in the backseat, and pumped gas, eyeballing the area, especially the pay phone that a young migrant worker was using. A small truck was parked nearby waiting on him, two guys in the cab and a mountain of cantaloupes in the back. After a few minutes, the young migrant hung up, got in the truck, reversed, turned around, and drove past the pumps and children in shorts milling around an RV with Ohio plates.

After sipping his coffee, taking a couple of minutes for safety's sake, Leo handed Herman the sunglasses. "Do it now. Quick."

Herman opened the back door, reached out a shoeless foot. "Why don't we use that cell phone you have, the one from the hospital?"

"Call me paranoid, but do you want to risk them tracing you? Go, Herman."

He looked like a vagrant shuffling over to the pay phone with bare feet, tugging up beltless pants, cap jammed over his head, and rocking those ridiculous shades.

Leo got back into the car and drank his coffee. Smoked his first cigarette of the morning, musing on events—what he'd done and how this day might come back to hurt him, even though the reason he'd acted in the first place was to stop past events from hurting him.

Herman returned to the backseat, looking almost cheery. "Esteban says he will come this afternoon. He will fly to Tampa, from Tampa he will rent a car, you know? To pick me up."

"You told him to buy a map?"

"*Sí, sí.*" The old man clasped his hands.

Leo started the car. "Wait a minute. He said what time?"

"In the late afternoon, must be. His plane arrives at noon."

"Yes, but we need a time. So that when he comes we'll know it's his car at the gate."

"You want me to call him again?"

Leo gave the parking lot the once-over, saw cars pulling up at the pumps, truckers and pasty-legged tourists streaming in and out of the store, the place getting busy. "On second thought, forget about it. Too many eyes, making me kinda nervous."

They pulled out and headed north on I-75 again. Leo made damn sure he glued the needle to the speed limit. They passed the last exit to Sarasota and then Bradenton, open stretches of land on both sides, now and again the glimpse of a low ranch house behind a fence in the middle of nowhere that made Leo feel lonely.

Miles and miles of monotonous highway. Herman fell asleep, woke up, dozed off again. Leo smoked a cigarette, put the radio on. Daydreamed.

Near the exit to Parrish, Herman woke up and in the rearview, Leo noticed Herman studying him, like he was seeing him for the first time. "You are going to be a father. Congratulations. I wish I had children, but I never met the right woman. You want a boy or a girl?"

"I've been thinking about that, and I want to say it doesn't matter either way, just for the child to be healthy, but I'd be fooling myself. I want a little girl."

"Why? You are a man. A man should want a boy, a son, no?"

Leo considered the question, staring at the road. "This man

wants a girl, that's all I know." He came around a curve, leaning into it, and said, "Because maybe men are no good. Most of the men I know are simply no damn good. No insult to you, but it's true. And all the women in my life are like saints compared." Check that. Sometimes he didn't know what to feel about his mother.

"Any one, boy or girl," Herman said, "makes you a lucky man. You must believe that."

They lapsed into a comfortable silence for a few miles. Then Herman commented on the weather, wondering what it would be like in New Jersey, if it was snowing. The weather was always a fallback conversation topic, wasn't it? But Leo wanted to talk about something that had been pressing him for the last fifty-odd miles. With his exit in sight—Sun City Center, Exit 240—he finally asked the question: "Herman, why are they looking for you?"

No sound from the backseat.

"You don't have to tell me, of course. But seeing as how I'm the one bringing you all this way . . ."

"I get votes. For candidates. Just a job I do. For people like your brother. For this, now, they want to kill me."

Leo shook out another cigarette from the pack on the seat. Held the cigarette between his lips and stared at Herman in the rearview. "No one's going to kill you, Herman. I promise you that. This shit is going to end today. You believe that?"

"I *want* to believe it."

Leo lit the cigarette, looked at himself in the mirror, squinting in the smoke. Thought he looked real cool, began to *feel* cool. "That's right," he said. "Damn straight."

20

THE LITTLE LADY BEHIND THE DESK at the apartment office said, "Yes, dear, they're gone. Sorry to tell you. Tessa came in here and paid the rent, said she was coming back before the end of the month for the rest of her stuff. That car was loaded with clothes and boxes and whatnot, and that dog they have? Barking in the cage like a crazy person. I felt sorry for Tessa, she looked so frazzled. Don't know where her boyfriend was. What's his name again?"

"Leo," Celina said. Knowing the lady was testing her, giving her the up-and-down, Celina standing there in her silk blouse and conservative black skirt and low heels, smiling back at her.

The lady peered over her reading glasses. "And you are . . . her sister, you said? You don't look anything like her."

"No, I'm Leo's sister-in-law. So she didn't say where she was going? No forwarding address?" Celina's hands rested on the handle of the gift basket she'd put on the desk. "I mean, it would be a pity if she didn't get this."

"Well, as I said, I'll give it to her when she comes back."

"The only thing is, what if she comes back late at night, when the office is closed, you know? It's not like it's priceless what's in here, but it would mean a lot to her. Just some baby washcloths, bath towels, Balmex for diaper rash. And champagne to celebrate because a little bit of alcohol is great for let-down if you're breast-feeding, and I happen to know Tessa *so* wants to breast-feed. No chance at all I can leave it in the apartment? I'll be really quick."

"Sorry, dear. I can't do that."

Celina put on a pout. "That's too bad. But maybe I can leave a note, slide it under her door? That's allowed, isn't it?"

Five minutes later, Celina was standing in front of the apartment door, her most bendable credit card in her hand. She knocked on the door firmly, just to be sure. Nothing. She knocked again, to be absolutely sure, the sound echoing down the empty hallway. She slid the card into the crack between the door and the frame as far as it could go, tilted the card toward her until it was almost touching the doorknob, pushing it again until it slid in some more. She bent the card the opposite way, forcing the lock to pop back, and quick as that, she opened the door and stepped in.

"Honey, I'm home," she said and closed the door, holding her breath, listening for sounds.

The apartment smelled of dog. Boxes were stacked up near the sofa. A half-empty cup of milky coffee sat on a side table next to a plate of crumbs. She moved into the kitchen—no notes on the fridge. She glided through the living room, looking for mail. There, in a pile in a basket on the floor. She flipped through the envelopes, nothing but junk mail and utility bills. The bedroom was a disaster, sheets tangled, clothes strewn across the bed. And more boxes. She opened them: clothes and women's shoes. She rummaged through drawers of clothes: nothing valuable there. Under the bed she found a shoe box with a Ziploc bag of marijuana seeds and stems.

In the walk-in closet, behind long dresses hanging from the rack, she found a heavy wooden filing cabinet. She opened it, and smiled.

It took her about two minutes of rifling through old IRS forms before she struck gold. An ordinary manila folder with neat handwriting across the front: *Wimauma house paperwork.* There were a bunch of envelopes inside. The second one gave her what she wanted. A page in it read: *Hillsborough County Notice of Ad Valorem Taxes and Non–Ad Valorem Assessments.* Under that was Tessa's name and a Wimauma address.

Celina fanned herself with the envelope, smiling—she couldn't help it. She looked around the room, a room in somebody else's home, and felt so deliciously wicked it made her horny.

21

L EO AWOKE FROM A DREAM and for a few seconds didn't know where he was or whether it was morning or evening. He was lying on the tattered cushions of a pine sofa. Bare yellow walls. A low-ceilinged living room. Breeze whistling through tears in the window screen, puffing through a screen door. Two empty cans of Chef Boyardee ravioli on a table in the living room.

He remembered now: He and Herman had arrived around midday, hungry and sleepy. In a kitchen cabinet they found the canned foods that Tessa had brought on one of her cleaning trips. They left the white albacore chunks and Vienna sausages for later, opened the ravioli, got two spoons, and dug in, straight from the can. They washed lunch down with tap water.

Afterward, Herman fell asleep in the master bedroom in the back that was all clean and fresh-smelling, the bed spread with new linen that Tessa had bought. The other bedroom was jammed with trunks of her dead aunt's stuff, broken furniture pushed against the walls, old appliances blocking access to the closet, windows with dusty curtains pulled tight, the room stuffy and haunted-like. Leo had stretched out on the living room sofa.

He forced himself up now and padded barefoot through the

house, peeked in on Herman. Still sleeping, mouth open. Leo
toured the house, noting the latches on the double-slung windows, where all the doors led, and which ones had deadbolts,
like the one that opened onto the front porch. They had entered
through the side porch door; it seemed that the front door wasn't
used much. He tried the keys Tessa had given him. None worked
on the front door.

He cranked open the glass louver windows in the living
room, looked out at the grassy front yard. Three towering
oaks laced with Spanish moss partially shaded the dirt driveway that snaked around from the gate of the wood-and-wire
fence.

He went out into the yard, enjoying the coolness of the grass
and dirt under his feet. Smoked a cigarette. Felt the sun on
his shoulders, his hair. Said to himself: Listen up, Leo. Let's get
this plan straight. First, you're going to make sure Herman
drives away safely with his nephew. Then you're going to that
Wal-Mart you passed back there on State Road 674, phone
Tessa, and give her the good news. Then you and she can start
your new life. Then you'll be free. Free to enjoy your life together and live happily ever after, no Patrick around, no more
Lonesome Point talk to disturb the peace.

Tell yourself the truth, man. You think happily ever after's
going to happen? He sucked on the Marlboro and pitched it on
the ground. Stepped on it with his bare feet. Damn right it's
gonna happen. It occurred to him, staring at the Spanish moss
shifting in the breeze, the high grass by the fence bending,
that settling down finally with someone, starting a family, was

his retreat from confusion. The confusion that was the Varela family.

Tessa, I love you. Baby whose name we don't know yet but who will be gorgeous and bouncy, I love you, too. Because you're giving me back my sanity and something to live for.

But would the guilt keep hanging on?

One day, he was going to tell Tessa everything. She probably knew by now that he was no poet. Shit, to publish a handful of things in little journals nobody reads was not the same as finding your calling. The only real calling he ever heard was the guilty whisper in the back of his mind, telling him, for years now, that he was just like his family. That deep down he was a coward all these years for knowing about the Rev, the Rev's stolen car, and not telling a soul.

It was time to let all that go, though. Time to do the right thing. He couldn't go on living like this. Raising a family, teaching your baby girl to do right, knowing you had the chance to do right yourself and never did—maybe Patrick could live that way. But he was not like Patrick, and he was proving it now.

He walked around the yard, occasionally swatting at sand fleas. He thought he could smell the earth from the fields they had passed down the road, where migrant workers were picking strawberries. The only other residence they'd seen on the road was a run-down trailer park, a gravel lot, no fence, signpost, or mailbox out front. You passed beat-up pickups and cars, rust-stained trailers, then not until a mile and a half later you came upon a wire fence covered in vines, this yard in the shade of oak trees, and this farmhouse with two porches, set far back from the dirt driveway. He and Herman were isolated here, the rural underground. They were going to be safe, they were going to be safe, they were going to be safe. . . .

22

W HERE?"

"Wimauma. I'll spell it. W-i-m-a-u-m-a."

"How did you find out?"

"I did what had to be done."

"Where are you, Celina?"

"Well, I'm lying down on their bed. In their bedroom, which smells kinda doggy, if you ask me, and I'm thinking about you. About us."

Patrick walked down the hall and into his office and sat down in front of the computer. "We'll see right now if this is the right address. What's Tessa's last name again?"

"Woodson."

Patrick scratched the name on a piece of paper. He said, "Wimauma, Wimauma . . ." Typing *Wimauma, Florida* into the Google search window. He hit Enter, and a list of sites popped up on the screen. "Hillsborough County," he said. "You still there?"

"I'm here."

"Bear with me," he said and cleared the search window and typed in *Hillsborough County Property Appraiser.* Hit Enter. Once in the appraiser's Web site, he clicked on Property Record Search and tapped out *Woodson Tessa* into a box and selected to sort results by name. "Got it." He read the address to her.

"It's a match."

"Celina, I couldn't ask for better than this."

"I could. I'm lying here all alone in this empty room. Wouldn't you want to do it in somebody else's house? Ever had that fantasy?"

Patrick shifted around in his chair. "You're a bad, bad girl."

"Am I a bad girl? You want to punish me?"

"I want to give you a spanking."

"I can help you with that. Listen. I'm raising my skirt now. Can you picture it?"

He pulled his nose away from the screen and sat back. "Keep talking naughty, see what happens to you."

"You want me? I want to hear you say it."

"I want you, bad girl."

"I want you, too. I did this for us, I want you to know that. A woman's got to do what she can to protect her family. Her man. You're *my* man. It's the least a bad woman can do for her man."

"I can't tell you how much I appreciate this."

"Why don't you show me, this afternoon?"

Patrick was getting excited, smiling, picturing his wife naked on the floor, right there by the desk, on her back, long black hair fanned out on the carpet.

23

BERNARD WAS SWEATING HARD in his bedroom. He'd knocked out one set of twenty reps of shrug-bar dead lifts at 380 pounds, banged out two punishing sets of one-arm dumbbell rows, eight reps of 120 pounds being all he wanted today, and now it was on to the main course: lifting the Blob.

The Blob was a sawed-off half of an old York cast-iron 100-pound dumbbell. Back in the seventies, a man named Richard Sorin was the first to lift it with a one-hand pinch grip. In fact, for inspiration, Bernard had a poster on his wall of Sorin lifting the Blob in a cluttered garage gym, hands all chalked up, wearing those short shorts from back in the day. Gripsters all over America worked toward this feat. Bernard was almost there. He'd succeeded a couple of times, sweating, forearm veins popping, getting that cast-iron sucker a few inches off the rubber mat, before his grip gave out and *bam*, he had to drop it.

The man in the apartment below had complained to the rental office, but Bernard didn't give a fuck and continued his training. Then one day he met the man in the second-floor laundry room. He approached the guy, something telling Bernard to go with brain and not brawn, so he apologized to him for the noise, because he just didn't realize sometimes when setting down his wife's wheelchair how much of a racket he was making, but he was going to try his darn best from now on to be a little more considerate of his neighbors, though it was hard, his wife needing all the help she could get since losing her leg to diabetes, you know?

Mr. Sanchez—"call me Luis"—never complained again.

Bernard dried his hands on a towel and powdered them with a handful of chalk from a bowl on the dresser. He clapped his hands and sent up a white puff. The only thing on the mat now was the Blob. That evil, grip-tearing, old-school iron bitch. Bernard said, "All right, brother," and bent over and slapped a wide pinch grip around it. He squeezed hard, psyching himself up for the lift, when the phone on the nightstand rang. It kept ringing and ringing and annoying the fuck out of him and killing his concentration, until finally he hollered, "Mona!"

No answer for a few seconds. Then his wife shouted from the living room, "Who you screaming at?"

"Sorry." His voice softened. "Get the phone for me, please?"

It stopped ringing. He heard Mona talking, then she said, "It's for you."

TWENTY-FIVE MINUTES later, Bernard had showered and shaved, both head and face, and was dressed in a blue Perry Ellis shirt, a ruby red tie, and black slacks, all of which Mona had ironed to help him make that daily transformation from Bernard to Big B.

He went into the living room to say good-bye to her. He could see just the top of her head over the back of the chair, where she sat in front of the TV ten hours a day. The box was on, Dr. Phil smugly talking down to some weepy white woman,

people in the audience nodding like bobble heads. Two baskets
of laundry were on the sofa, a pile of clean folded clothes, a por-
table writing table with a checkbook, pen, bills, and a couple of
pill bottles. Mona was diabetic but she still had both legs and
would've been able to walk just fine if it wasn't for her severely
arthritic knees and the fact that she weighed 310 pounds—at
least that's what she told him, always talking about her weight
but not wanting to do shit about it, always finding excuses. She
rarely left the apartment and preferred to travel the rooms by
wheelchair. Bernard was through trying to persuade her to go
outside, walk around the parking lot for exercise. The woman's
problem was in her head. But, man, he loved him some Mona.

He kissed her on her clammy forehead. "I gone, boo."

"Okay, luscious. I'm gonna roast that pork with some pinto
beans and collards for later when you come home, hear?"

Bernard checked himself in the little mirror by the front door,
tightened his tie knot. The thing he was most proud of in his adult
life was sticking to his vows, until death do him part from his
Mona. Despite the fact she was probably too big a woman, he'd
never once strayed. How many men could boast like that? Self-
discipline—that's what made him feel justified every day to dress
sharp in these expensive threads that Mr. Rocha made his people
wear, that made the transformation from Bernard to Big B complete.

FREDDY LIVED on the fifth floor of an old apartment building
on Collins Avenue in Miami Beach. As run-down as the place
was, it cost him plenty, but since Rocha had taken over from

Parra, the future looked about $300 a month rosier. So Freddy had decided to stick it out a little longer, the view of the Atlantic just sweet enough.

Right now, though, he wasn't feeling too positive. From his balcony he watched Bernard walk across the street toward the building. He threw on his tie, hurried to the door.

Bernard came in saying, "Man, I busted like three red lights to get here. What's this little situation?"

Freddy was halfway across the living room carpet to the bedroom, knotting his tie. "Goddamn if I didn't overdose the bitch."

Bernard said, "What?" and followed him through the double doors, and then the two of them were standing at the foot of the bed staring at a naked white woman prostrate on the rumpled sheets.

"The fuck happened here, Fred?"

"A wee bit of a problem," Freddy said, taking a watch from a night-table drawer, "is what we have here."

Bernard looked from Freddy to the woman and back.

"Tourist from Scotland," Freddy said, grinning. "Man, I couldn't resist. After that fiasco last night? Shit, a man got to have something to ease his worries." He started tucking in his shirt. "Met this one this morning at that hotel down the beach, poolside. We got to talking over brunch. Got to drinking a little bit, Bloody Marys, you know how it is." He rummaged through the drawer. "Man, where the fuck my cuff links?"

"So like"—Bernard lifted his shoulders and threw up his hands—"what happened? She all right, she gonna live? What's she on?" He walked to the side of the bed, reached down and felt her neck for a pulse.

"Roofies, B, chill. That's it. And maybe a little kush I been saving that we smoked, but aside from a couple Bloody Marys by the pool, it's roofies got her like this."

"I feel a pulse. Faint, though."

"I need you to help me get her dressed. We walk her out to the back stairwell, carry her down. Or we could try the elevator, prop her up, but that's too risky, that's why I'm thinking the stairs, get me?"

Bernard checked his watch. "Not like we got much time. It's like a three-hour drive to Wimauma, right?"

Freddy stopped fiddling with his cuff links. "You going to lecture me about time now, Bernard?"

"All I'm saying . . ." Bernard shrugged. "Forget it. What you want me do?"

Freddy plucked a red bikini bottom off the carpet and dropped it on the bed, followed by a bikini top, a wispy sarong, a white T-shirt. "Help me put on her clothes first."

Lifting and tugging here, holding up an arm or leg there, they dressed her in rough fashion.

Perspiration beaded Bernard's forehead. He had the woman propped up, sitting half slumped forward, and watched Freddy get his shoes from a walk-in closet, shoehorn them on. "Man, I thought after last time shit like this happened that was it, Fred."

Freddy checked himself in a wall mirror. He said, "B?" catching Bernard's glance in the mirror. "I don't want to hear it, all right?"

They carried her down the musty, carpeted hallway to the stairwell and down the stairs, five fucking floors, Freddy thinking, Was this pussy worth it? Sweating up your nice Kenneth

Cole shirt like this? He had to laugh at himself. Getting a little taste the easy way was hard work. Although he'd have a good story to remember later, to jack off to.

They hit the second-to-last flight of stairs and Bernard said, "You smiling but I don't find this funny no way. This woman ain't nothing petite."

Okay, Bernard was irritated, Freddy thought, knock it off and look serious.

Luckily, there was no one walking along the first-floor hallway, no one in the lobby. They sat her up, slouching to one side, in a wraparound leatherette chair. A woman dozing, waiting on a friend. Freddy positioned her sunglasses on her head and slipped her sandals on her feet and that was that. He was rid of her. On a one-to-ten scale, she was a seven, this one, with round bubble tits that maybe could bump her up to a seven and a half, an ass on the flat side, but you can't get everything in life, let's be realistic. He'd always remember those puffy nipples and the brown freckles that dotted her arms and legs and just below her belly button and above that fine red-tinged bush. You go, Fred.

24

THROUGH THE HEAT WAVES at the rest stop on I-75, Patrick saw the black Mercedes coming. He stood by his Porsche, hands in his pockets, dressed just casually enough. Loose jeans, black T-shirt untucked, low-cut hiking boots. No telling what to expect out there in the sticks.

The Mercedes rolled up and swung into the space next to his, Patrick lifting his chin in greeting at the two men inside. He heard the doors unlock. He opened the door behind the driver and climbed in.

The men turned around in their seats. Freddy Robinson, who had hardly aged, and the shaved-head driver, Rocha's bodyguard from the barbershop meeting. Freddy did the introductions. Patrick said, "Gentlemen," and buckled up, dispensing with handshakes.

Freddy gave him a grin. "Mr. Patrick fucking Varela, the son of Belize that has risen to conquer the Miami political scene. It's good to see you after all this time, brother."

Patrick inhaled the air-conditioning deeply and exhaled the bullshit. "Let me tell you something, Freddy. This is no pleasure trip for me or you. Am I right? I'd suggest we be businesslike about the day's unpleasantries, and if we're lucky, we won't even need to see each other again. What do you think?"

Freddy's grin faded. He looked away for a second. "How you

gonna say that to me now when we're like family? I always re-garded you like a brother, you know that?" He studied Patrick, frowning. Then he chuckled. "Man. I'm fucking with you." He shook his head and turned around to the front. "Uncouth moth-erfuckas like me enjoy that kinda shit. Of course we'll keep this *business*like. I'm all about *business*like. Now, if you want, later on, you can be businesslike and be the one pull the trigger. How about that?"

Patrick said, "Bernard? Whenever you're ready."

Bernard turned to the wheel, dropped the car in reverse.

Patrick said to him, "Mr. Rocha spoke to you?"

"That's right."

"So you understand I'll be directing you?"

"He said you the man with the directions."

"Excellent. Then let's get back out on I-75 and head north to Exit 240. Any questions?"

Bernard looked at Freddy, then at Patrick in the rearview. "None at all."

"Then," and Patrick sat back, "let's go and get this over with."

Bernard headed north. Freddy adjusted his seat belt and pushed in a CD, horns-heavy jazz.

Two tracks down, he swiveled his head around and said to Patrick, "What kind of music you like? Smooth jazz? Old-school R&B? I know you ain't no hip-hopper. So like what? Barry Manilow?"

Smirking, eyes agleam with playfulness the way they used to be when he was sixteen. Patrick broke off the eye contact, checked his watch, and gazed out the window at the dense vegetation behind the fence of the Big Cypress Preserve, bright green in the heat. "Play whatever you want."

"I'd put on the radio. National Public Radio." He knitted his eyebrows and said in an anchorman baritone, *"All Things Considered."* He pointed at Patrick. "Want some of that? We could listen to the burning issues of the day. Engage in some deep intellectual conversation. Right here, me, you and my man Big B."

After a moment, Patrick said, "You know, that's a great idea. Why don't you put that on?" Looking straight at Freddy.

Freddy let a few seconds pass. "Guess what?" He turned to the front. "Just remembered this radio can't catch that kinda station," and he cranked the jazz higher, the confusing blare of saxophones filling the car.

IT WAS a long, boring drive. Patrick eventually dozed off and woke up near the Port Charlotte exit, looked around, and dozed off again. He opened his eyes to see the St. Petersburg exit up ahead. He felt alert and calmer than he expected. Freddy snapped off the music and started paying closer attention.

They exited at Sun City Center and headed east, slowly, only about four miles to go. A retirement community. Senior citizens driving along frontage roads on golf carts. Golf carts everywhere, and old people in hats. Strip malls on both sides with Walgreens and CVS, Pizza Hut, Wendy's, McDonald's. A little city with one major road smack in the middle of nowhere. They continued on State Road 674, past a Wal-Mart Supercenter, into Wimauma.

"South of the border is what this is," Freddy said, looking around.

Mexican men in straw hats ambled along the roadside. Store-fronts everywhere in Spanish. MARTA'S TACQUERIA. LA TIENDA DEL PRIMOS. A little ways farther and an old wooden building, EL PEQUENO MEXICANO FOOD RESTAURANT. That one gave Freddy a chuckle. Old pickup trucks and cars crept along in front of them, veering off without indicating into dusty park-ing lots. Migrant workers sat in the bed of a truck drinking Cokes outside a *supermercado*.

"When we pass back, remind me to stop for some tortillas, B," Freddy said. "Uh-oh, look who's coming up the road. Slow down, B."

Bernard eased off the pedal as the state trooper rolled by, and Freddy gave him a stiff-palmed Queen Elizabeth wave.

Patrick said, "Did you have to do that?"

"Just being a good citizen, Commissioner."

A couple of miles outside Wimauma, they wheeled right and headed south. On both sides of the road, men worked vast straw-berry fields in the sun, running up with full buckets and dump-ing berries into the bed of a truck, running back between rows of green plants, past other men stooped over and picking furi-ously.

Then more fields, private dirt driveways, a long stretch of wood-and-wire fence, a dilapidated trailer park, and there it was. Leo's farm. The Mercedes pulled up facing the gate. Bernard lowered the windows and the three of them sat there quietly, listening.

"Well, well," Freddy said, "welcome to the Honeycomb hideout. The backwoods. The boonies. The redneck-infested swamps."

Patrick said, "Let's go inside, then."

Freddy turned to the backseat. "I guess you want me to get out and open the gate?"

Before Patrick could summon a retort, Freddy was out of the car. Patrick watched the absurdly overdressed Freddy saunter through knee-high weeds to unlatch the gate. Patrick said in a low voice, "Bernard?"

"Uh-huh?"

"Mr. Rocha spoke to you and you understand completely everything that needs to be done this afternoon. Do I assume correctly?"

Bernard nodded. "Yes, sir. I've got things covered."

Freddy opened the gate wide and stood to the side, hands on hips. "Smell that green freshness in the air. That's a country smell, boy. Country living ain't for me but you can't beat that smell."

Talking too loudly for Patrick's comfort, considering that the farmhouse was no more than fifty fucking feet from the end of the dirt driveway. Inside the house, they probably had already heard the car, and now with Freddy's yapping, the slim chance of surprising them was gone. Patrick turned to Bernard. "Let's do this thing quick."

Bernard stomped the gas, tires kicking up dirt, and the car raced up the driveway and braked hard at the back bumper of a blue Camry. Bernard hauled himself out the door, Patrick sprang out of his, and Freddy circled to the back of the house, a small pistol in hand, looking for a back door that might provide an escape.

But there wouldn't be any; Leo and the old man would not

escape the consequences of their irresponsible behavior. Patrick was pretty sure of that now.

LEO HAD heard the car approaching. He'd gotten up from the sofa and walked over to the window, thinking finally Herman's nephew was here. Then he saw Freddy at the gate.

It took Leo's brain a second to process what he was seeing. Absorb the truth that it was really Freddy out there in his necktie and shirtsleeves, opening the gate for the black Mercedes.

He backed away from the window. Turned and raced toward the master bedroom, shouting, "Herman, Herman," slapping the walls with his good hand to rouse the old man. Herman wasn't in the bedroom or the bathroom. This was all happening too fast. Leo ran back down the corridor. He shouldn't have fallen asleep just now.

He found Herman trying to jam himself behind a trunk in the storage room closet. Herman said, *"Están aquí,"* and Leo hooked him by an arm and tugged him out. The window was a no-go, a jumble of chairs and a huge armoire blocking the passage. They ran down the corridor to the master bedroom. Leo said, "Look. We're going through that window. Don't be scared." He led Herman to it, holding his hand like a child's. "We're going to climb that back fence and run through that field in the back, you understand me?"

Leo reached out to reassure Herman as they edged toward the window, and Herman clutched Leo's upper arm, bony fingers squeezing. Right then, Leo felt an overwhelming kinship with the old man. Saw fear in Herman's eyes, his face pale.

Leo opened the window locks, slid the bottom panel up.

The old man was trembling. Leo squared up to him and held his arms down by his sides. "Don't be scared. I'll help lower you out of the window. You grip my forearm here, right here, real tight. I'll lower you down to the grass. It's about a foot drop after that. Don't move from there until I climb out. C'mon, now." He turned Herman to the open window. The weedy yard, sagging wire fence, the overgrown field stretching into the distance.

Herman poked his head out to see for himself and pulled back inside, shaking his head.

Leo patted his shoulder. "You can do this, you've got to. We don't have time."

Herman gestured absently at the window and he sort of sighed, giving up.

Leo pushed his head out.

Freddy was standing in the yard, smiling, aiming a pistol at the window. "Good afternoon, my good buddy." He launched into off-key singing. *"It's a beautiful day in the neighborhood, a beautiful day in your neighborhood, would you be mine, could you be mine. Won't you be my neighbor, and invite me inside your cozy cottage, before I cap your ass good."*

Leo pulled his head back inside and slammed the window panel down. Freddy was wearing a grin, all distorted through the windowpane now as he shouted something inaudible.

Looking through the glass at Freddy, Leo stepped backward, turned on his heels, and stalked out of the room, down the corridor and into the kitchen. He could hear Herman shuffling behind him.

He rummaged through the kitchen drawers until he found just the thing in a clutter of dinner knives: a small black-handled paring knife. Edge dull as a church sermon, but it would have to do. A backup to the Swiss Army in his back pocket. He lifted his pants leg and slipped the knife deep into his right sock, tucked it behind his ankle bone.

He heard footsteps on the side porch, glimpsed a big shadow cover the window, then Bernard bringing his hands to the sides of his face and peering in.

Somebody knocked on the door, and how Leo knew this he couldn't say, but he knew it was Patrick. He could *feel* his brother there.

"Don't be afraid," he said to Herman, who was standing in the kitchen, looking lost. "We'll get through this, we'll get through this." Preparing his heart for any kind of violence. Clenching his fist for it.

25

L EO UNLOCKED THE DOOR and stood next to Herman.
Patrick walked in, all calm and serious. His eyes passed over the two of them and then took in the room. He came closer, fixed Leo with a withering stare, and shook his head. Bernard entered.

Seconds later Freddy barged in, whistling, no gun in his hands now. "Love what you've done with the place, Lee. Don't think I like your manners, though. You couldn't have invited us in on your own? Got to wait for a man to ask? And what," looking around the room, "no drinks for the guests? Where's your hospitality?"

Patrick threw him a look. "Freddy? Shut the door, then be quiet for a couple minutes." He stepped over to Herman.

Herman's hand was trembling. He licked his lips, eyed Patrick. *"No he hablado con nadie, Señor Varela."*

Patrick shrugged. "I don't expect you to say otherwise. But if it's indeed true you haven't talked, we need to make sure it remains that way."

"Que tu quieres decir con eso?"

Freddy's eyes were boring into Patrick's back when he said, "Could you speak some fucking English, please?"

Leo saw Patrick close his eyes a second, trying to be patient with this guy he still clearly detested. Leo said, "You're not touching this man, Patrick. I won't let you hurt this man."

Patrick raised a finger. "Shut up. Shut the hell up. You think you're in any position to tell me what you're going to do?"

"You're getting carried away with this. I know why you want this man, I know, all right? But if he promises you right now he won't talk, he means it. No need to hurt him."

"What do you think, that you're the good guy? The protector of the downtrodden and the oppressed, some bullshit like that? You're naïve, Leo. Step aside."

Leo pointed at him. "I came to you telling you about Freddy with your best interest at heart. Now look at this. You and him together . . ." and Leo stepped forward, lowered his voice. "Patrick, I'm asking you to reconsider this."

"You came to me with *your* best interest at heart, buddy. You're trying to make out you're the good guy here? Do I really have to remind you about the kind of man you are?"

"No more killing, Patrick. No more! You want Herman, you'll have to deal with me."

Patrick folded his hands down in front of him and smiled, the young arrogant Patrick all over again. "You fool. You think you can go back and change the past? This is not about guilt. This is not about doing good in the world to right the wrongs of the past or whatever the hell you're thinking. This is about my career. About what people have invested in me being at stake."

Leo gestured. "Come on, asshole. Come and try me."

Patrick said, "You're talking big because you think we won't hurt you? That's why you're challenging me? Well, surprise,

surprise, Leo." He looked over his shoulder at Bernard and beckoned him with a tilt of the head.

Leo saw Bernard coming and balled his fists, angling his body and setting his feet to begin swinging if necessary.

Freddy stepped from behind Patrick and aimed his gun at Leo's chest. "No time for heroes today, baby."

Bernard was all over Leo, seizing his shoulder and spinning him around to face the wall. Leo swiveled his head to the side, saw white plastic zip-ties in Bernard's hand, felt the big man bend back his right wrist, pain streaking up his arm, and he dropped all ideas of struggling.

Bernard tied Leo's wrists behind his back.

Patrick said, "I don't want to hear anything else from him."

Bernard turned Leo around, whipped out a strip of black cloth, and pressed it tightly across Leo's mouth, parting his lips with it, tying it off behind his head.

His wrists burned where the zip-tie pressed into the skin, his lips hurt from the gag that had pulled his face into a grimace. He wondered how ridiculous he looked. He stared at Patrick, then his eyes started watering, and he looked down at the floor.

Patrick was saying something to Herman, and Herman kept repeating, *"No he dicho nada a nadie,"* voice rising and getting shrill.

Patrick went down the hall and into the bathroom. He returned, said to Freddy, "Take the old man. Put him in the tub and do what you have to do."

Freddy said, "And him?" nodding at Leo.

Patrick said, "Give me a minute on that."

"Mr. Rocha broke it down to me, that you'd be the one making that call, but I'm just saying, don't get sloppy—given the fact this is my ass on the line, too, feel me?"

Patrick said through his teeth, "Take Massani in there and gimme a fucking minute, Freddy."

"Look, you don't have all day to decide. I ain't standing by for you to wave no magic wand about my future. Leo ain't got the balls to keep quiet? Then we got to do what we got to do."

Bernard said, "Oh, shit, what's this, now?" and moved toward the back porch window.

Through the open louvers, Leo could see that a white car had pulled up at the gate and a man was getting out of the driver's side. Now the man was walking toward the gate. Curly hair, thick mustache. Sportcoat and jeans.

Freddy looked at Patrick. "See what I mean?"

Patrick turned to Herman. *"Quien es el?"*

Herman shrugged. *"No se."*

Patrick said, "Bullshit," and motioned to Bernard, then crossed to the side of the window and peeked out.

Bernard wrapped black cloth tight across Herman's mouth, the old man's eyes wide, darting at Leo. Bernard led Herman to the side of the window next to Patrick. Patrick looked at him. "Nod if you know that man."

Herman stared at Patrick. Nodded.

"A relative?"

Another nod.

"Brother . . . son . . . nephew . . . Nephew?"

Patrick turned to Freddy. "You need to let this fellow know

he has the wrong house. I'd tell him myself, but considering I'm a known entity, I would prefer not to."

"At your service," Freddy said. "Shit, all's you gotta do is say the word, Commissioner Varela." He grandly flung out his arms to adjust his sleeves, then unlocked the side door and sauntered outside.

The room was silent as they watched Freddy talking to the man at the gate. Freddy pointed this way and that, nodded. Pointed again, made a circle in the air with a finger.

Leo watched the scene, feeling disassociated from it, thinking—of all things—about how much Esteban out there resembled Kotter from *Welcome Back, Kotter.*

Two minutes later, Esteban stuffed a piece of paper in his pocket and got back into the white car, reversed, and was gone.

Freddy was opening the door, stepping back into the house, when Bernard said, "What the fuck?"

The white car had returned, rolling to a stop in front of the gate. Esteban was getting out again, looking at the house, frowning.

"This dude's pissing me off," Freddy said, then spun around and headed back to the gate.

Through the window, Leo saw Esteban studying the piece of paper when Freddy came up to him and started talking. Esteban shook his head, waved the paper at Freddy. Freddy looked off to the side and made a face, said something else, and started walking away. Esteban reached down and tried to unlock the gate. Freddy ran up, shouting at him, but now Esteban had opened the gate and was pointing at the house. Freddy put a hand on

Esteban's arm, tried to lead him back to the car. Esteban yanked his arm away, getting mad. Leo could see the vein in his neck.

Patrick said, "I don't like this. Bernard, you might have to take over."

The old man started fidgeting next to Bernard.

Outside, Freddy and Esteban were arguing nose to nose now. Esteban pushed Freddy in the chest, Freddy stumbling back.

Patrick said, "Get out there, Bernard. Now."

Freddy slapped Esteban, and Esteban swung at him, barreling into him, the two of them toppling, out of the line of sight. Bernard hurried to the door while Patrick leaned in to the window, trying to peer around the wall.

Two shots echoed, everybody in the room flinching.

Somebody outside screamed and another shot went off.

Bernard ran, feet pounding down the porch. He raced past the window, out the gate, and stopped by the car, head snapping left and right. Then he wheeled to his right and was gone from view.

The old man started a low moan. Tears were streaming down his face, his lips twisting around the black cloth.

"Shut the hell up," Patrick said, flustered. "Just *shut* up."

Leo watched him and slowly lowered into a crouch. He waited, watched Patrick craning his neck to look around the corner. Leo's right hand found his pants cuff, slid it up. His fingers touched the knife handle. Gripped it. How would he do this? Saw away quickly, leap up, put the blade to Parick's throat? Man, he had to try something. He pulled up the knife, inch by inch, watching Patrick. The old man kept sobbing. Leo was sweating. Shit, the blade had snagged on his socks.

Patrick came away from the window, cussing under his breath, and Leo shoved the knife back into his sock.

The door flew open, Bernard lumbered in. Freddy followed, nearly panting, clutching the pistol, grass in his hair.

Patrick said, "What happened?"

Bernard shook his head.

Freddy said, "We lost him."

"You *lost* him? Did you shoot him? What the fuck happened?"

"Slow down there. Yeah, I shot him, shit. Got him right in the neck but I don't know why he didn't drop."

"He ran through the bush across the road there," Bernard said. "We went in, couldn't see shit. So I tell Freddy let's not waste no more time, better we bail, get this job done and go home."

"Well, it's plan B, then," Patrick said. "Go look in his car, grab the keys if they're in there and let's get moving. Goddammit, Freddy."

Freddy canted his head and looked at Patrick. He stuck the pistol in his waistband, all defiant.

Patrick stormed past. "The dude didn't believe me," Freddy said, but Patrick wasn't listening, already at the door. "Was arguing with me and saying he was going to call the police. What am I supposed to do, be polite?"

Patrick turned and said, "You better blindfold them." Jerking a thumb at Leo and Herman.

Bernard patted his pockets. "With what?"

Patrick stopped. "What do you mean? A length of cloth or something."

"I'm out. Freddy . . . you bring?"

"Don't look at me."

Patrick sighed, put a palm over his forehead and massaged his temples. "Then I guess you'll have to take the ones off their mouths and use those, correct? Jesus."

Bernard removed the gags and blindfolded Herman, the old man's head bobbing around like a rag doll's when Bernard knotted the cloth, then he turned to Leo.

Leo said, "You don't have to go through with this, Patrick."

"You hear me asking your opinion?"

"Herman is giving you his word. He hasn't talked to anybody, won't talk to anybody. Give the man a chance, what's gotten into you?"

"Keep on talking and I swear to god I'll kill you right here. You know what your problem is, Leo? You don't know whose side you're on. You know too much, you've seen too much. You've *done* things. Time to wake up and accept who you really are."

Standing there blindfolded, hands tied behind his back, Leo could feel his brother examining him.

Patrick said, "The last of the innocent men. That's who you think you are?"

Then Leo heard Patrick walking away.

OUT IN the yard, the breeze chilled Leo, and he realized he was sweating heavily. Bernard pushed him forward. Being blindfolded seemed to sharpen his senses—he smelled the grass as he walked, the dirt, and picked up a whiff of leather when they opened the car door; heard parakeets chirping in an invisible tree somewhere on the left.

He heard Herman say, *"Por favor, Señor Varela, no me mates."*

Bernard said, "Ho, shit, look at this. Old man pissing himself here."

They were about to get into the car, but they stopped.

"I can't have no piss in my ride," Freddy said. "This shit's leased."

"For chrissake," Patrick said.

"For chrissake nothin'. Your ass ain't the one have to clean the car, Mr. Commissioner."

Herman said, *"Por favor, caballeros. . . ."*

Leo heard a sigh. Heard Patrick say, *"Quitate tus pantalones, Herman."*

"Cómo?"

"Tus pantalones. Quitetelos."

Leo heard movement in the grass, a zipper. He pictured the old man in drawers, bare feet in the grass, skinny toes.

"Long as his shirt ain't wet," Freddy said, "he could go ahead and wrap it 'round, cover himself."

Patrick said, "How very considerate of you."

26

THEY LEFT FINALLY, Leo in the backseat leaning a shoulder against the door, Herman jammed in the middle, Patrick at the other door. Bernard rolled to a stop at the intersection of two dirt roads. Overgrown fields on all corners, no homes or people in the vicinity. Bernard said, "Where to?"

Patrick leafed through the papers in his lap. "Says here . . . let's hang a right. We're going straight for point six miles. The place is supposed to be on the right."

"What place is that?" Freddy said, turning around slightly to Patrick.

Patrick shook his head over the stupidity of such a question in the presence of two men whom you had just blindfolded in order to disorient them and prevent them from knowing where they were. Was this man a perfect ass or what?

"Here?" Bernard leaned forward, slowing the car down. "What's this sign coming up here say?"

Patrick inhaled deeply for patience. Sweet Jesus. He was with Mutt and Jeff now. He snapped his fingers, getting Bernard's attention, and lifted a finger to his lips.

Bernard stopped the car in front of the roadside sign, about three feet high and partly covered by weeds. COMMERCIAL PROPERTY FOR SALE—19 ACRES. CALL 813-555-3357.

It was the site of an old fish farm that Rocha had told him

about, five miles southwest of Wimauma; property Rocha had considered buying months back and knew was still unsold. He'd explained it would serve the purpose of the trip just fine.

Patrick said, close to Bernard's ear, "This is it. Supposed to be a break in the fence some yards up you can drive through."

The car crept forward. Patrick prepared himself.

LEO WAS trying not to panic.

They turned right and bounced along a rough road. After a minute, the car rolled to a stop. A front door opened. Somebody got out. Probably Bernard. Then a back door opened. Somebody else got out. The doors slammed shut.

From up front, Freddy's voice: "Listen to me good, Leo. You're my dawg and like I told you from the start, we into a serious business here, kind where nobody's indispensable. This is like a power game here, like chess, Monopoly, or whatever, but for real. Real dollars, real blood. It should be crystal to you by now that you shut your mouth, you'll get out of this okay, this got nothing to do with you. Understand? Don't flap your gums, keep . . . Hold up, they're calling me."

A door opened, closed with a thunk, and Leo sat in the blindfold darkness, the car still running. He felt Herman pressing up against him and smelled leather seats and urine in the icy a/c.

"BERNARD," FREDDY said, handing him the pistol. "The show is yours."

With two hands, Bernard held the gun barrel-down, eased

the slide back, checked the chamber. He pushed the gun into his waistband behind his back and walked over to Patrick, who was standing in the knee-high grass examining the landscape. Insects buzzing in the heat. Wild grass everywhere. In the distance, a concrete-block pump house with a green fiberglass roof. Broken iron frames over rows of overgrown fish ponds. A rusting hulk of a tractor heaped beside a trail.

Bernard said quietly, "Waiting for the word."

Patrick did not turn around. He took a deep breath and shut his eyes. He nodded.

Bernard pivoted and strode to the car. He opened the door, grabbed Herman by an arm, and brought him out.

Herman said, *"No, no, por favor. No me mates, señor."*

Bernard ignored him and led him through the grass in the blazing heat. Herman stumbled, fell to his knees. Bernard hauled him up. "Leo," Herman bawled, *"ayudame."* He started crying, Bernard pulling him along.

Bernard said, "Come on, don't be a baby about this." He looked back at Freddy. "You coming?"

Freddy raised his eyebrows. "What, you want me to hold your hand?"

"I'll need you to hold this man still when we get there. And then it's good if somebody else can check see I did this thing right so there's no argument from nobody."

Freddy sucked his teeth, shaking his head. He turned to look at Patrick.

Patrick said, nodding seriously, "Makes sense."

Freddy said, "Sheeet," looking away. Then, "Whatever, man, let's do this," and he motioned for Bernard to lead the way.

Bernard pushed Herman forward, the old man shouting:

"*Señor Varela, no me mates!*"

PATRICK STOOD with arms folded, staring into the far-off stand of oak trees, a few tall cypresses mixed in with them. He refused to look at the old man shouting like a fool. There was a loud thud from the car. Another one. Patrick looked over his shoulder, saw the car rocking. Another thud, the Mercedes shaking. Another thud, and a window buckled.

Patrick went over there and poked his head through the driver's door. "All right, Leo, cool it."

Leo was half lying on the backseat, rearing a leg back for another kick, face red and sweaty. He misjudged and kicked the door. "You can't kill that old man, Patrick. Let him go, let him go!"

Patrick straightened and looked over the roof at Bernard and Freddy taking the old man behind some oak trees. "This is basically a done deal, Leo. Now it's time for you to accept it and work with me."

"You don't have to do this," Leo said. "What kinda person does murderous shit like this?"

Patrick opened the rear door wide and said, "Let's go, Leo. Let's come outside for fresh air."

Leo shook his head, lying back, hands behind him, face to the ceiling. "No way I'm going anywhere with you. You want to kill me, you're gonna have to do it right here, or drag my ass out, pick one."

Patrick angled his body into the doorway. "Kill you? I want to talk to you. Sit up."

Leo didn't move.

"Where's Tessa, Leo? I need to know."

Leo didn't reply.

"I need to know where Tessa is because I need to be sure she doesn't talk to a soul about what happened at Lonesome Point. Believe me, I know that she knows, because I know you told her."

Leo was shaking his head.

Patrick said, "What? You saying you didn't tell her?" He laughed. "Ridiculous. I know you told her because I know you. I *know* you. Where can I find her so she and I can have a sit-down?"

"Go to hell, Patrick."

That pissed Patrick off. He said, "Get up," tapping Leo's leg. "Come on, get up." Leo would not move. Patrick dropped a palm on Leo's lower leg to tug him out. Leo drew his legs back fast and kicked, Patrick pulling back and catching one on the forearm, one thumping him hard on a shoulder.

"Get away!" Leo bicycled his feet, stamping at air.

Patrick stepped back from the door and took a deep breath. He opened the driver's door and jacked the trunk release. He went to the back, raised the trunk lid and returned to the door. Leo had lifted his head off the seat, breathing heavy, neck muscles taut. Listening hard, trying to figure what was coming next.

Patrick counted off in his head one, two, three, ducked in and snatched Leo's ankles, and hauled him forward, Leo flopping back and kicking but already too far outside, then Patrick yanked him by the belt and out he came, head hitting the doorframe, body tumbling onto the grass. Leo said, "Ahh, fuck, my shoulder," and Patrick didn't let up, grabbing his arms, twisting him onto his stomach, straddling him, and pushing his face into the grass. "Okay, now," Patrick said, breathing hard. "Let's talk." He pushed Leo's face down. "What's that? You say you can't talk, your mouth's full of dirt?" He lifted Leo's head by the hair. "That better?" He slapped the back of Leo's head. "Where's Tessa?"

Leo turned his face to the side, dirt all over his nose and the blindfold. He blew his nose sharply. "Take these things off my arms, motherfucker, and let's see what happens to you."

Patrick punched him in the back of the head. Punched him again. "Where's Tessa?" He had his fist cocked to slug him again, but controlled himself. Keeping a tight hold on Leo's wrists, Patrick lifted himself up. He said, "Get on your feet." Leo staggered up, Patrick wrenching his wrist back just enough to cause some pain. Leo tried to fight back, twisting wildly, but he was blind and off-balance and Patrick muscled him over to the trunk. He spun him around and said, "Sit down," pushing down on Leo's shoulders. He put a palm over Leo's chest and said calmly, "Let's rest here a second so we can talk, okay?" and Leo seemed to relax, lifting his blindfolded face, as Patrick pushed him with two hands, Leo falling backward into the trunk, legs flying up, one foot sticking out of the trunk. Patrick brought the lid down on the leg firmly, it pulled back, and Patrick slammed the trunk shut.

He leaned both palms on the car, trying to catch some air. He turned his face to the side and wiped his forehead on a sleeve and stared at his sweaty reflection in the rear window.

Leo screamed. The car rocked. Another scream. *"Patrick!"*

* * *

BERNARD TOOK the old man down a trail behind a dense thicket. Freddy was scouting another trail to the right, an overgrown one, to see where that led.

Herman had clawed the blindfold off with one hand. It didn't matter much to Bernard if that's how the old man wanted it, the end was going to be the same. Why would any man want to see one of the worst things that could happen to him? Anticipation was the most painful part. Everybody would prefer to go in their sleep, right? All peaceful, so you don't hardly feel the pain. It was only humane to help a man in this predicament by offering a blindfold, but if he didn't see the need, then granting him a clear-eyed view was the humane thing to do, and Bernard considered himself humane, on a basic level.

He'd never done a job like this out of animosity or for kicks. This was strictly a job, a thing that required doing efficiently and professionally, and goddamn right he was a professional.

"Slow down, old boy, where you think you going? Stay in front of me."

Herman tottered through the bush, his bony shoulders heaving as he sobbed, the shirt tied around his waist making him look even more pathetic. Bernard felt sorry for the old guy, but this was a thing that had to be done, and it was just that simple.

From somewhere behind him, Freddy said, "Everything too much in the open back here. Keep pushing on, B."

After a row of weed-choked ponds, the trail leveled and veered off into the bush. They picked up another trail to the left, a two-track that snaked past heaps of engine blocks and tires strewn by the ponds. This trail petered out near a cluster of oak trees, heavy bush behind that. This was as perfect a spot as any.

And Herman sensed it, too, because he took off, lurching to the right and crashing through the grass, jangly like a skeleton.

"Wait up there, now," and Bernard made four big steps and snatched him by a shoulder and yanked him back, the old man flailing backward and toppling to the ground.

Freddy laughed.

Bernard shook his head at the old man. "Damn fool." He hoisted him by an arm and kept a hand on his shoulder to stay him. "What you doing, *señor*? Calm yourself. Don't act like this, losing all your dignity. I hear that you a respectable gentleman in your community. This ain't no way for a respectable man to act, running hysterical like this. It's disgraceful. What . . . what's the matter?"

Herman was stomping his feet. He bent over and swatted at his legs. Red ants were crawling over his feet and up his legs. Bernard pulled him out of the high grass, stooped down and brushed off the ants. He took his handkerchief and knocked off the ants, while the old dude held on to his shoulder for support.

Herman moaned his approval and quit fidgeting. When Bernard stood up, he was sweating. Freddy looked impatient. Bernard beat the kerchief against a thigh and wiped his brow with it. "Got to help out a man in his last moments," Bernard said to Freddy. He handed the kerchief to Herman. "Go ahead. Dry your face. Can't stand to see you crying like that."

Herman wouldn't take it, mumbling something in Spanish and turning his face away.

Bernard folded the kerchief and stuffed it back into his shirt pocket. "Man, you're making this harder than—"

Herman was off for the races again, running north this time, back along the two-track, shouting in Spanish.

Freddy said, "Yo, give me that fucking gun."

Bernard threw up his hands. "See, now, this some *bull*shit," and he chugged after Herman.

Herman left the two-track, and the ground seemed to give way under him and he pitched forward, disappearing in the bushes. Then came a splash.

Bernard reached the pond as Herman was grasping at grass tufts, trying to pull himself out of the muck, waist-deep. He was soaked, hair plastered on his skull. Bernard stood at the edge of the pond and watched. The man was naked, shirt floating among the weeds. Opening his mouth to say something, no sound coming out, eyes pleading. He raised a hand to Bernard.

"Just look at you," Bernard said. "Shameful," and he dragged the pistol from his waistband and held it down by his right leg.

PATRICK LISTENED to Leo bumping around inside the trunk. "How're you doing in there? Terrified yet?"

"Let me out, please. Please let me out."

Patrick said, "Nothing would please me more than to release this lock, get you out standing next to me in this cool, wonderful fresh air. But I can't do that with you acting like an idiot. I'm sure it must be steaming in there, positively *steaming*. And you being all claustrophobic, it must seem terribly dark in there, huh, Leo?" He listened to Leo hitting the trunk. "You're ranting, you're losing control, so I need you to calm down and help yourself. Tell me where Tessa is and I'll let you out. I promise you, tell me where I can find her, I'll open this trunk."

"Please . . . please just let me out, man!"

"No, no, you're not paying attention. Tell me where Tessa is, Leo."

"Why? Let me out, please."

"I think you know why."

"Patrick, I can't breathe in here."

"It's because you're so claustrophobic. You must feel like you're suffocating. Must be pure hell in there." He listened to Leo kicking the trunk. "Where is Tessa, Leo?"

"I don't know. Jesus Christ, just let me out."

Patrick released a long breath. "See, I just don't believe you. You're not being honest with me, but I'm going to be honest with you right now. I intend to make sure she doesn't talk to anybody about Lonesome Point, I'm not going to lie to you. I know that you told her everything about me but you left out the rotten stuff about yourself, didn't you? You told her everything about what *I* did, but you, you probably came off looking like the noble pothead."

"Everything that happened back then was wrong. It was wrong. Please, man, let me outta here!"

"Aw, listen to you, *it was wrong,* you and your petty moralizing. Too late for that now, don't you understand that? You've forgotten what side you're on, you've forgotten the number one rule of this game? Silence. Keep your fucking mouth shut. Keep your guilt to yourself."

The car rocked as Leo moved around. *"Open up. For fuck's sake."*

"Where is Tessa, Leo?"

"I'm not telling you. You think I'm stupid? If I tell you, you'll kill me and then you'll go and kill her." Leo kicked the inside of the trunk. He made a barely audible sound, groaned. *"Let me the fuck outta here and get it over with."*

Not good. His voice was stronger, had lost that edge of panic. Patrick leaned hard on the car. "You know what? You're right. I *am* going to kill you. But you have a choice. You could roast in there a bit longer and let your claustrophobia fuck with your mind. Or speak up now and I'll let you out into some fresh air and get it done for you quickly."

No reply.

"Did you hear me?"

"If Tessa doesn't hear from me by five o'clock, she'll call the police and report me missing. They'll go to the farmhouse to check."

"Is that so? Well, we aren't there, so why worry?"

"She'll say that the last person she saw me with was you. If I go missing, the police will be coming to speak to you. Tessa'll tell them everything."

Patrick pressed his palms against the car. His chest felt tight and he couldn't breathe. He sucked in air through his mouth and let it out slowly and evenly. Did he have a choice here? If he released Leo and he ratted, so many people would go down, not to mention him losing everything he'd toiled for all these years, plus his freedom. Voter fraud conspiracy would get him at least a year, probably more. And what about kidnapping and false imprisonment?—which was what this was right here.

And murder? Absolutely no way he was going to let this all slide beyond his control. His reputation tarnished, his career shot. His family embarrassed. Scandalizing his firm and his associates along the way, then him going to prison—his mind was racing.

Patrick rested his forehead on the trunk. He had a massive headache, a hollowness widening in the middle of his chest. "The offer has been withdrawn, Leo. I have nothing more to say to you except one day we'll meet on the other side. Because you and me, we're going to the same place."

27

L EO WAS SUFFOCATING. He was baking. Dying slowly. He was just thankful for the blindfold. At first he thought he was going to lose control of his thoughts, his sanity, but breath by breath he understood that claustrophobia wasn't that frightening to a blind man, and Patrick talking outside actually made it easier, didn't make him feel so trapped.

Terror lurked at the edges, but he tried not to make that his focus, busying himself, trying to believe that it wasn't futile. All the while Patrick was talking to him, he was sawing away with the paring knife at the zip-tie around his wrists. He was drenched in sweat, twisted in a painful semi-fetal, having freed the knife from his right sock and manipulated it in his right fist so that once out of every three attempts the blade bit into the plastic and gave him a little hope.

His shoulder burned, the back of his head was sore, his fingers ached. His lungs felt stuffed with cotton. The car moved with the sawing. Once again he said, sawing, "Please, man, let me out," just to distract Patrick, kind of cover up what he was doing.

He kicked the car for good measure, sawing away, car rocking. A part of him wanted to believe that Patrick hadn't made up his mind. The weird thing was that even as he was working that knife, gritting his teeth, he felt comforted that it was Patrick standing outside there, his brother, not Bernard or Freddy, but his own blood, who might still give him a chance. He shouted, "What exactly do you want me to do, Patrick? Act from now on like any of this never happened?"

No response.

"Talk to me, Patrick. Don't run away from the truth."

"What do you know about the truth, Leo? You spent half your life clouding your brain, running away from reality, writing shit poetry nobody reads, and then you're thinking, Oh, poor me, what do I have to show for myself? No career to speak of, no money in your pocket? All that, that's your own fault. Don't blame anyone but yourself for your problems."

"All right, all right . . . just don't hurt Tessa. Promise me that. She's pregnant. Don't hurt her."

No response.

"You can't give me that, at least? She's *pregnant*, Patrick."

"Shut up, Leo."

Leo could feel the cut in the plastic widening under the blade. A slow, torturous process, this cutting. Like filing away at a mountain. But as long as he was doing something, he could scale down the panic. The heat wasn't so bad, and he could still breathe, see? He wasn't suffocating. He was in control. A tad dizzy but that was the heat . . . but the heat wasn't so bad . . . damn, he wasn't making any sense. He stopped to rest, breathing with his mouth open.

The part of Leo's heart that wanted to believe in his brother's goodness was dying with every breath in this sweltering trunk. Now he felt like he was running out of air. He said, "Oh, man, oh, man . . ." His head dropped to the side against the plasticky-smelling carpet, and he rested for a minute. As soon as he freed his hands, he would pop that trunk-release lever he knew all these newer cars had. He needed to do this fast, before he passed out.

The knife slipped out of his grasp. He was so drained he didn't bother trying to fumble around to find it. Not yet. He was thinking about how Patrick had revealed nothing new about himself today. Leo had always known, deep in the mental gutters where you left the dirtiest, most subversive, most dangerous questions, he'd always known there was something disturbingly wrong with Patrick. How could a brother not know? Patrick was missing a conscience, an empathy gene, something. He was too ruthless to be anything else but a sociopath, a narcissist. Some months back, Leo had been wondering maybe he and Patrick would close their distance, patch things up, that maybe Patrick did love him, but he saw now that he had been delusional.

He found the knife again, positioned it, his left shoulder bruised, fingers cramping. After a breath, he returned to work. He began playing a game with himself: Fifty strokes would set him free. If not, then between sixty and seventy-five. Let's see if he was right—go.

There was a *pop pop pop* from outside.

28

THE OLD MAN FLOATED naked in the shallow muddy pond, face turned slightly to the side. Red mess in the white hair.

Freddy stood at the edge of the pond. "Poor motherfucker. This some cold shit, boy, what we do here is some cold shit." He *tsk-tsk*ed. He looked off into the bush and rubbed his hands together. "Okay, then, we came, we saw, and this and that, so let's head back to civilization."

Bernard led the way back. They passed under the oak trees to where the path gave out and they swished through grass for a distance. Bernard stopped suddenly amid higher grass and Freddy almost walked into him. They were at the edge of another pond. Bernard tilted his head toward it.

Freddy stood beside him and looked down. "What?"

"See anything in there?"

"Mud and water, Bernard. Let's go, dawg, what the fuck?"

"You don't see like your future down there?"

Freddy squinted at him. "Boy, you crazy," and turned to leave.

But Bernard slapped a hand on his shoulder and held him there. Freddy tried to move, but it was not happening.

"What up—what the hell you doing, B?"

Bernard had slipped that big hand up to his neck and was

squeezing. Squeezing hard, now with two hands. Freddy grabbed Bernard's wrist. He tried to speak, made a small sound at the back of his throat, punching at Bernard's arms, swiping and clawing his face one time.

Bernard smiled and kept the pressure on, Freddy's eyes bulging, mouth open. Bernard leaned all his two hundred ninety pounds into it, Freddy buckling under the force. Bernard saying, "Fuck you, you rapist," pressing his thumbs into the windpipe, "no respect for women, fucking rapist," Freddy's arms flapping, falling to his side, "you get what you deserve." It was so easy; Bernard didn't expect this to be so easy. He didn't want to enjoy this, but, damn, he was enjoying this shit. His grip was brutal, brother, no doubt about it, Freddy's eyes just about popping out of his head, face changing colors, reddish brown to a purple hue. He was close to passing out. His arms stopped moving, body going limp.

Bernard didn't want to look anymore. He shut his eyes and choked that neck harder to hurry things. For some reason, the Lord's Prayer floated into his head, he began remembering whole lines of it, even though he hadn't remotely thought about praying in years. But this up-close job, the first he'd ever done with two hands, had him tripping in a big way. Our Father, who art in heaven, hallowed be—there, that was it—something snapped and crumpled under his thumbs, and he held on for just a moment longer, making sure it was over indeed.

He released the neck, the body dropped. "Thy will be done, thy kingdom come." He opened his eyes, saw the body twisted in the grass, and moved away. "Thy kingdom . . ." He was breathing fast. He took a moment.

What was all this religion shit doing in his head? His brain was going electric. He fumbled with his handkerchief, saw a tremor in his hand. He wiped his face and spat to get a foul taste out of his mouth. Why'd he have to go and use his hands like that? Probably despised Freddy more than he had realized. A secret hatred that must've been building and building.

He didn't want to reflect on this anymore. He hurried over to Freddy, bent down, trying not to look, grabbed the ankles and dragged the body to the edge of the pond, then heaved it in. It splashed on its side.

The last thing he noticed before he walked away was that Freddy had soiled himself. Bernard trudged up the trail, feeling queasy.

PATRICK WATCHED him return alone, half-moons of sweat under his arms. He waited until Bernard was nearer before he asked, "The verdict? That was kind of quick."

Bernard barely looked at him, raising two fingers and walking past, toward the car. "Two men currently dead."

Patrick watched him open the front passenger door and rummage through the glove compartment and come away with a small bottle of Purell. He squirted some into a palm, tossed the bottle onto the seat, and walked up to Patrick, rubbing his palms together.

"Mr. Rocha said there'd be a monetary token of appreciation for this particular thing, which to me was a nasty job. Therefore I'd be in the right to expect some solid appreciation. If you want to just be a gentleman about it."

Patrick said, "No arguments here," and reached deep into a

pants pocket and handed over a wedge of folded hundreds. "With much gratitude, Bernard."

Bernard thumbed through the bills, lips moving as he counted silently. "Don't mind if I do." He shoved the money into his back pocket. He nodded at the car. "Didn't see dude in the backseat. He in the trunk, huh?"

"Was the best place for him. Most soundproof spot, if you understand." Patrick walked over to the car, gestured at the windows. "He almost kicked out the glass. Freddy was here, he would've taken a shit."

"Freddy took a shit, believe me. So what we doing with this dude?"

"Well," Patrick said, slapping hands together and folding them. "He's not giving me anything." He stared at the trunk for a long time. Somewhere in the bushes a bird started to sing. The heat was growing unbearable. He sighed, looking around and up at the sun, which was sinking, wisps of clouds, the heat unforgiving. "You need me to say it?"

Bernard wiped his bald head with his kerchief. "Truthfully, I need you to say it. 'Cause it's, well, that's your brother in there." He folded the kerchief. "I know this ain't no easy thing. I mean, me myself, I just been through some horribleness back in the bushes there that blew my mind, kinda makes a man don't want to go through that shit no more if he can help it. Therefore you have to give me the word for certain, to the point where in the back of my mind I know a hundred percent I'm doing what you really desire, you get me?"

Patrick lowered his head and pinched the knot between his

eyes and massaged. "Yes, but that's my dilemma. I don't know if I want to give you that word right now. I'm of the mind that we best hold on, see if we can convince him to give up his fiancée. It might take twenty minutes. An hour, maybe." Massaging his brow, waiting to see if Bernard accepted that.

"You know, Mr. Varela?" Bernard looked off at the trees. "All due respect, time ain't a luxury we have. That man Freddy shot might still be running around out there, and the risk is me and you get sent up, and I been in lockdown before and that ain't no cakewalk, either. What I'm trying to say now is you please consider the risk."

"You're right." Patrick took three steps closer to the trunk and stared at it. "You need me to say it, then I will. You got the green light, okay? But you'll have to take care of it. Wait, before you say anything," Patrick raising a hand without turning to look at Bernard. "I will compensate you again. Handsomely."

No response came, and the silence crept on. Patrick turned around squarely.

Bernard said, "See now, you're talking *at* me. Assuming that I'm doing it. Like I already agreed. I don't remember accepting this particular job."

Here is where Patrick needed to be careful, but firm. "I'll give you double what's in your pocket there, but if you don't like that, then can you please hand me the fucking gun, Bernard? Because I'm not in the mood, and because I find it really unseemly to haggle over the price of somebody's life." Patrick came up to him and stretched out a hand. Bernard didn't move. "What? Change of heart, Bernard?" They locked eyes.

Eventually, Bernard's face creased into a smile, and he nodded, saying, "Okay, then, okay." He stepped around Patrick and moved to the car.

Watching him, it occurred to Patrick that he was right all along, that after today the person most detrimental to his career would be Bernard right here, the man who would know all the incriminating details. Always, always, there had to be a loose end, a wrinkle to iron out, somebody to silence—it just never fucking ended.

This was why Patrick was carrying a small .45 automatic in a Milt Sparks inside-the-waistband holster belted tight to the flat of his right hip, under his shirt. As soon as Bernard returned, Patrick would finish the matter forever. Let the big man stroll back, feel comfortable. Patrick would step behind him, put that three-inch barrel at the base of his smooth head. A .45-caliber to the brain is so sudden it must be painless, could hardly rank as cruel.

29

L EO HAD HEARD MOST OF IT: They were talking about him like he was a foregone conclusion. But his arms were free now. He'd cut through the zip-tie, slipped the knife back into his right sock, alongside his ankle bone. Transferred the Swiss Army knife from his front pocket to his back pocket.

His panic had burned off and a calm had settled in. If he was going to die, he'd do it with no fear, no tears. And if he saw even a ghost of a chance, he was going to fight back. What choice did he have? He nudged the blindfold down, breathing low, preparing his mind.

He blinked into the darkness and immediately started second-guessing himself. As soon as the trunk opened, they'd see the blindfold off, see his hands free, and shoot him right away. He didn't stand a chance if he didn't act quickly. Come out swinging. Or maybe bide his time? Wait till they escorted him to some secluded spot, then . . .

He laid his head back, taking in gulps of air. Man, he didn't know how much longer he could take this torture, the heat, the dank air. Keeping his phobia in check.

Light blinded him when the trunk flew open.

"Morning, sunshine," he heard Bernard say, but he couldn't see anything, covering his eyes. The fresh air chilled him. He blinked, catching shapes, forms, way too much glare.

Patrick said, "He got loose. How'd he get loose?"

"That's what I want to know."

Bernard's rough hands grabbed his arms and shirt and hauled him out, Leo stumbling on jelly legs. It hurt too much to open his eyes completely. Bernard whirled him around, patted him down fast, pulled the Swiss Army knife from his back pocket. He cussed under his breath and flung the knife away.

"Do it now," Patrick said, "just go off somewhere and do it now." His voice trailing away.

Leo was unable to see where Patrick was exactly but he knew it was somewhere on the right. Bernard on the left, close by. Leo raised a hand to shield his eyes. He glimpsed green all around, gauzy bush and the haze of trees. The air smelled like freshly turned earth. He thought of running.

Bernard grasped his left wrist, bent his hand back and cranked his arm straight up so that Leo had to lean forward, drop to his knees.

"Know how easy I could snap your arm in two?"

Leo said, "Pretty easy . . . I'd suspect," sounding much calmer than he was feeling. And right then he decided he was going to play it cool and wait for his moment. Be clever. Didn't know how he'd do it, overcome two of them, but he'd have to do it. Or never see Tessa again. Never see his daughter born. Because he knew it was going to be a daughter. He shivered as the air stirred around him. His Nadia. That was it—he had found a name. He liked the sound. Na-di-a. The poetry of syllables.

Bernard was saying, "Me and you going for a walk. When I tell you stop, you stop. When I tell you turn around, you turn around. If you run, it's game over. If you think you can resist, may the good Lord help you, you'll suffer before you sign off. Do like I say, when I say."

Leo's vision wasn't so blurry anymore. He said, "I understand."

Bernard stood him up, keeping a tight hold of the arm. Stooped at the waist, Leo got a look at his surroundings, streaks of orange in the sky, sunset in about an hour. He turned his head, saw Patrick by the car, facing away.

Bernard said, "Move," and Leo started walking, bent over like an old man, one arm pushed up high behind him, shoulder aflame, in fact all his joints hurting. They worked their way down a trail maybe twenty yards before Leo stumbled over a rock. Bernard was holding him with one hand, the other hand clutching—what? A gun? He'd heard what sounded like three shots when he was in the trunk but the only gun he'd seen was Freddy's, back at the farmhouse, and where was Freddy?

That's when it came to him, what Patrick planned.

Freddy was dead. Leo knew this, instinct was telling him this. And the reason was Lonesome Point. His vision sharpened as he tottered on, bent over. He thought, Well, Leo, at least you've gotten over your claustrophobia. And now you're going to die. If he didn't act soon, he knew that in a few minutes he'd be dead.

AFTER THE trail rose and leveled off, they started along another one on the left and passed engine blocks rusting in the high grass, then a series of ponds.

Leo said, "Wait. I need to throw up."

Bernard kept steering, moving him along. "Then do it, it don't matter to me."

"Oh, god," Leo moaned. "Just stop, give me a second—let me throw up, then you can do what you need to do, that's all I'm asking, man," Leo using his best acting voice.

Bernard's grip eased, then he released him. Leo groaned and rubbed his wrist and lowered himself into a crouch, head bowed. He saw a trail of ants crawling from a mound, through the grass, heading toward a pond, and he remembered one cool morning when he was a kid, maybe seven, sitting on his haunches like this, examining insects in the grass, mysterious black bugs. He must've watched them for hours.

Bernard had a gun in his hand now, Leo noticed. He was holding it low, in his right hand.

Leo moaned again. "Bernard, just one more thing." He spat between his legs. "Why you think my brother came on this trip? The man's a politician. A public figure. He didn't need to come."

Bernard stepped close behind him. "The fuck you saying?"

"I'm saying as soon as you finish killing me, my brother'll kill you."

Bernard chuckled. "You don't think I already figured that? A politician, huh? Cool, but I ain't no politician, I been playing these here games since I was fifteen, so don't worry about me."

Leo spat thickly to the left, reaching down with his right hand, up under his pants cuff, fingers pulling at this sock, touching the knife handle.

Bernard said, "Now, next time you open your mouth, I better see vomit flying."

Leo turned his body so that it blocked the view of his right hand drawing the knife out of his sock. Rising slowly out of his crouch but head bowed like he might puke at any second.

"So tell me, son," Bernard smiling, "how is your politician brother going to kill me?"

Leo liked that—keeping Bernard talking—so he replied fast: "With a .45 I know he carries. See, the thing is, you have the guts to shoot me but he doesn't, seeing as how I'm his brother. But he's got the guts to pull that .45 soon as you turn your back, no problem." Leo's head up now, eyes on the black pistol moving as Bernard said, laughing, "Ho, shit, I'd like to see him try," and Leo said, "He'll do it fast," springing at Bernard with the knife, aiming for the throat, his other hand batting the gun down. The blade sank into the side of Bernard's neck, and Leo pulled it out, blood spewing, drove it in again, as the gun exploded painfully loud beside him. He and Bernard stood chest to chest, and Leo stuck it in again and again, this time in the jaw, then the neck. He'd pinioned Bernard's gun hand under his arm, held it tight, while he tried to pull out the knife, but it was stuck in Bernard. The gun fired, again, then again, Bernard stumbling away, leaning to his side, the gun gone. He pawed at the knife in his neck. Blood everywhere.

Bernard dropped hard on his knees. The knife jutted out of his neck, lodged just under his ear. He twisted his head, leaned his body down, pulling at the handle but having no luck. It was slippery, the blade buried too deep. His mouth was open when he fell. He lay on his side, one hand on the handle, the other under his body.

Leo ran, heading south away from the car. Then he stopped and ran back, searching the ground. He found the pistol and shoved it behind his back and took off south again.

He went along the trail until it ended and he was in heavy

brush again. He trudged up a slope, then down through rows of dried-out ponds. He had no idea which direction led out. He was looking for a fence, something that marked a boundary. Beyond that he might find a road—he hoped. He came to a grove of young, scraggly live oaks, tried to figure a way around it. Thought maybe it was best to just push on through.

The first gunshot sent birds fluttering out of the trees, and Leo scurried into the grove. The second shot sounded closer, the round snapping over his head and splintering a tree trunk, and he looked up from the ground where he had thrown himself and saw Patrick running up, pointing the pistol and shouting, "You better stop there!" No more than fifty yards, running fast, and firing again.

Leo thought, My own brother is trying to shoot me. Trying to shoot me before I can get up and take cover behind all these trees.

He pushed himself off the ground, half crouching, tore deeper into the grove, swiping at branches. Snapping twigs underfoot, breaking the small branches. He heard two rapid-fire shots and something slammed into his left arm above the elbow. He said, "Fuck!" clasping the spot. It felt like he'd been whacked with a hammer, and it infuriated him. He ran on, jagged branches sticking him in the face. He wiped his forehead, and his hand came away smeared with blood. Blood rolling down his left arm, dripping on the grass and pelting leaves and tree trunks as he ran.

So this was what it felt like to be shot. Like a flame burning through to the bone. He tugged the pistol from his waistband at the same time a shot ripped over his head. Way too close. He was so scared he couldn't say if he was thinking right, but turning around, like he was doing now, pointing the gun at the man trying to kill him, no matter that it was Patrick—it felt like the only thing to do.

Through the weave of leaves and branches, he saw Patrick stepping up holding his own gun with two hands, and Leo raised the pistol and leveled it on Patrick's chest. He didn't think Patrick could see him. His arm was shaking, the gun sight dipped and lifted, Patrick advancing, closer. But Leo couldn't, he couldn't. He tilted the gun a fraction to the left and squeezed off a shot, the recoil startling him, the ground in front of Patrick kicking up, Patrick diving. He cowered under his arms and curled up, trying to make himself a smaller target.

Leo fired another shot wide, then turned and ran, leaving Patrick on the ground. He stamped and cracked and scraped through the trees. Stepping into a hole, twisting his ankle and falling; bounding up and falling again. He got up hobbling. He broke through the grove and stumbled into a green field, rows of endless green.

Long neat rows of strawberry plants. The air heavy with a sweetness. Strawberry rows hundreds of yards in front, to the left and right. In the distance, maybe half a mile ahead, a two-lane road.

Patrick was coming. Leo could hear branches breaking, bushes rustling. No attempts at being stealthy. Everything in the open now. No more deceptions, no more games, just this confrontation.

Leo couldn't expect to be safe running through this field. There was no cover; he might get shot in the back. He and Patrick would have to shoot it out. That was becoming clear as he stood there waiting, feeling sick, stomach twisting.

He started backing up, watching the trees, gun held straight out. He kept backing up, wide steps, and for a moment, an insane moment, he thought he'd make it home safe. But—what home? And would it ever be safe? He heard rustling, saw Patrick inching out from behind a tree.

Leo knew he was in a bad spot. When he saw Patrick's gun rise, he dropped and a shot sounded. Lying on his chest, he fired back without aiming. He didn't want to kill Patrick, but he sure as shit didn't want to die. So there it was.

And Patrick was coming now, and it didn't even look like him anymore, gaunt and sweaty, and that frightened Leo as much as anything. It was like this moment was unreal, some alternate universe, because these horrors did not happen to him. Patrick rushed out of the grove and fired two times before Leo could point the barrel properly. He finally shot, missing easily. Knowing this because there was Patrick standing about twenty feet away aiming at Leo's head and squeezing the trigger.

Nothing happened.

The slide on Patrick's gun was locked back.

The gun was empty.

Leo stood up. He trained the pistol on Patrick. Patrick fumbled with his gun, pulled out the magazine, and looked at it in disbelief. He stoned it to the ground and patted his pockets. Nothing there. He looked shocked. The gun slipped out of his hand and fell to the dirt. He raised a palm. "Wait," he said. "Listen to me, Leo."

Leo walked forward, finger on the trigger.

"You can't do this, Leo."

Leo felt shaky and weak. The pain in his arm was excruciating.

The sun in his eyes, he squinted and cocked his head. He aimed at the thickest part of Patrick's body, center mass. He stopped about ten feet away and said, "Take a step back. Go on, do it."

Patrick obeyed. "Please don't do this, Leo."

Leo motioned with the gun. "Keep going back until I tell you." He took a step forward for every one Patrick took backward. Leo stopped at the gun in the dirt and, keeping his aim on Patrick, he crouched and swiped it up. He jammed Patrick's gun in the front of his pants.

"Now . . ." His vision swam and the ground tilted. He waited for the earth to right itself. He said, "Now, this is the part where we say good-bye."

Patrick reached out, fingers quivering. "Come on, Lee. This isn't you. I apologize, Jesus, I'm so sorry, Lee, this mess, for everything, this whole mess got away from me—I didn't know what I was thinking—oh, Jesus, Lee, I've got kids, think about my kids. You can't shoot me like this, cold-blooded like this? Lee?"

Leo was shaking his head. His gun arm had stilled, front sight steady, about ten feet between him and Patrick. He could not miss.

"You're a better man than me, Leo. I—I don't know what else to say. What do you want me to do, beg for my life? Humiliate myself? Okay, look . . . please . . ." He sank to his knees, reaching out. "Put that gun away and let's talk, settle this"—he swallowed hard—"settle this like brothers. We're brothers!"

Leo spat into the dirt. "What I want you to do? I want you to go to prison. Somebody like you, you deserve a cold cell. But I'm thinking—"

"Put the gun down, please."

"I'm thinking I shouldn't even give you a choice. That would be too much of a luxury for somebody like you. I should end this right now, save you the embarrassment, the scandal, you know the rest. Maybe that's better for you," and he stepped forward aggressively, raised the barrel at Patrick's forehead.

"No!" Patrick threw up his hands, tossing his head to the side.

Leo felt cold in his heart. "What should I do?" He watched Patrick raising his head and weeping openly now. "Either way it's a gamble for me. I'll testify against you, you'll tell them things about me. But you can't prove anything and I'll talk about everything I know about what you're doing. So should I let the law take care of you? You might get off, right? You know how the justice system works. But if I shoot you, I could get caught, too, isn't that right?" His arm was shaking, fatigued. With his other hand, he held his wrist steady. "I have this little fantasy, about reciting a poem to you. It goes, 'This is the way the world ends, this is the way your career ends, this is the way your life ends, Patrick. Not with a bang, but with a whimper.'" He nodded. "Too bad somebody already beat me to it, you evil son of a bitch."

"Leo, please, you can't do this, this is not you, this is not you. . . ."

"You're wrong. This *is* me."

He fired.

Blackbirds fluttered out of trees in the distance to the east and flapped into the mellow blue. The shot seemed to ring in his ears forever.

He stood in the quieting field and looked up at the birds. Then a familiar fear took hold of him, and he turned and started running, running in the sweet air between rows of strawberries.

30

H E WAS SEVENTEEN YEARS OLD AGAIN, running fast. Nervous and exhilarated. Scaling a cement fence, a dog rushing at him, then scampering off when he kicked at it. He could see the car thief clambering over another fence. When he reached it, the boy had disappeared. One long street, a dog barking somewhere.

Leo and Freddy ran back to the Rev's Jag. Freddy stayed with the Jag while Leo drove around the neighborhood slowly in his father's car, leaning into the steering wheel, looking all around. He rolled down the windows, could feel his pulse in his ears.

He circled twice, ready to give up. At a house under construction on a corner, he saw something moving in the darkness. He reversed, turning so that his high beams spotlighted the house, the bushes, rebar sticking out of cement blocks.

The boy bounded out of the house and blurred through waist-high grass and leaped over the drain. Leo mashed the pedal and went after him.

He caught him full in the high beams, running, uncoordinated, looking back wildly, Leo shouting, "I got you now!" bulleting down the edge of the street.

He saw the boy turn, hands flying out. "No!"

Leo laughed, waiting, waiting for that last second to crank the wheel left, thinking he was going to make this thief shit his pants tonight, waiting as the car hurtled toward this wild-eyed boy.

What Leo saw most clearly was the blood. He also remembered the clatter and thump when the boy rolled over the hood, the thud against the windshield. He kind of recalled the boy falling off—that part seemed to take a long time.

Then he sat there in shock. Then, after a time, he stumbled out and knelt over the boy lying faceup in the middle of the street, blood leaking from his ears and nose. The boy still, not making a sound.

One open eye staring at Leo.

A light came on in the veranda of a house across the way. Leo nudged the boy's shoulder. "Hey, hey, wake up, hey," his voice catching in his throat.

He stood up, trembling, took himself over to the car, and sat behind the wheel. The engine was still running. There was a woman looking out from the veranda. Leo gripped the wheel, saw he had smeared it with blood; he looked at his hands, wiped them on his pants.

Headlights approached from up the street. It was Freddy, in the Rev's Jag. "I found Fonso. He's coming now."

More headlights rolled up. A police Land Rover, Fonso behind the wheel. Fonso parked on the grassy verge and he and Patrick got out.

Leo told them what happened. Fonso looked down at him, real cool, looked over at the woman on the veranda.

"Shit, I didn't mean to do it," Leo said.

"Easy there," Fonso said, checking out the scene. He smiled at Leo, calming him. "The police is here." He turned to Freddy.

"Keep on driving. Take the car to your house and stay home."
Then to Leo he said, "Go straight to Lonesome Point and wait
there. I got this. G'wan now."

Half an hour later, Leo was smoking a cigarette, sitting on
the hood of his father's car parked near the mangroves at the
edge of Lonesome Point. A faint wind was blowing. Heavy clouds
obscured the stars and the moon.

Fonso and Patrick stood in front of him, waiting for an answer.

Leo puffed the cigarette, tossed it away. "Well, what if we get
caught?"

Fonso said, "Get caught doing what? Didn't the police show
up? Cart the body away?"

Leo fired up another smoke, inhaled deep. "Who is he? What's
his name?"

"Just some thief."

"No, I need to know, I need to know. Who is this boy? I want
to *know*."

Fonso said, "I can't pronounce his last name, but his wallet
says Ramon."

"He's just a thief," Patrick said.

Leo lowered his head.

Fonso said, "We're trying to help you here, Leo."

Leo nodded, staring at the ground.

His cigarette burned down in his fingers.

Patrick said, "What're we gonna do, Leo?"

Leo tapped the long ash. He puffed the cigarette, flicked it
away, and stood up. "Let's bury his ass," he said. "Let's do it."

They lifted the body out of the back of Fonso's Land Rover

and carried it to a spot by clumps of bushes. They laid it down, oddly gentle about it, then Patrick brought the shovels, and they all started digging. The only sound you could hear was the shovels biting the earth, the wet clop of sand that piled up in a mound.

When it was deep enough—it didn't take that long—they lifted the body, Leo grabbing the feet, and dropped it in the hole. The boy's ankles were so skinny. Later on in his dreams, he'd feel them.

Moonlight peeked out of the clouds onto the clay ground.

They started covering the hole. Sand piled up on the chest, the legs. Sweat pouring off Leo, his shirt sticking to his back. Sand piling up. Even in the poor light, he could see the white of Ramon's open eye. He shoveled up a heavy load and pitched it over the face so that he wouldn't have to see it anymore.

31

LEO'S PACE HAD SLOWED to an ungainly walk. He kept his eyes on the road up ahead where the strawberry field ended. He was thirsty, so he stopped to pluck two berries and sucked on one. Spat the flesh out and popped the other in his mouth, continued walking. Eyes on the road. Heat shimmering over the bright green field.

His eyes were not focusing; the road seemed to be shifting, now up, now down. Maybe he was losing too much blood. Shit, his arm was on fire, the pain was killing him. The pain was killing him? He smiled at that. He spat out the strawberry but had no taste for another. He kept walking, unsteady.

When he looked back, Patrick was far away. Standing where Leo had left him. He was yelling something but was too far away to be heard. He was probably half deaf from the shot going off so close to his ear. The next time Leo saw him, he wanted it to be in a courtroom, then behind Plexiglas in a prison somewhere.

Leo stuck the pistol in his waistband, on the opposite side of the other gun. It was stupidly uncomfortable. Movies that made this look easy had misled him.

He came to the end of the field and saw that the road curved west to an intersection with what appeared to be a main drag about a mile ahead. On one corner was a gas station, a Shell, with a convenience store.

Cars were pulling in and out. When he saw one with sirens, he started running toward it, legs heavy. The car was black and gold, highway patrol colors, the car parked. Leo thought he was dreaming this. A trooper got out of the cruiser and crossed the road. Leo tried to pick up his feet. Running too slowly, through a wall of heat.

Two figures at the side of the road. An impossible distance. The trooper talking to a woman in a straw hat sitting in a chair under an umbrella. A roadside vendor.

It felt like one of those dreams in which he couldn't run fast enough. The road was a hundred miles. His feet flopped hard on the asphalt when he stopped, out of breath. He leaned over, hands on his thighs. His pants were soaked heavy with blood, his left arm bathed in it. His heart was racing, he needed to think straight. The guns.

He tugged them out and pitched them in the grass. He was going to keep on running, keep moving, before he collapsed.

He started off again. Then he felt himself lifting out of his body and he was one of those blackbirds that rose from the trees near the strawberry field and he could see Patrick standing below him, far down there in the field, and see the trooper, hat tipped low over his eyes, rapping a watermelon, and see himself running the road that narrowed and curved through farmland now, the smell of pesticide in the air. Was that Tessa over there, her belly big and beautiful, standing on the side in the grass? He thought he must be losing consciousness, his mind hovering just below the clouds, feeling that elation he used to feel when he was a boy, yearning, filled with hope; running this road that he'd been traveling for years, that had led all the way to this one afternoon, this moment, under a fading sun—all the way from Lonesome Point.

Leo just kept running.